T0160767

Elvis Presley Calls His Mother After The Ed Sullivan Show

ALSO BY SAMUEL CHARTERS

POETRY
The Children
The Landscape at Bolinas
Heroes of the Prize Ring
Days
To This Place
From a London Notebook
From a Swedish Notebook
In Lagos, Ereko Street, Nine PM
Of Those Who Died
A Note on the Varieties of Locust

FICTION
Mr Jabi and Mr Smythe
Jelly Roll Morton's Last Night at the Jungle Inn
Louisiana Black

CRITICISM
Some Poems/Poets: Studies of American Underground Poetry Since 1945

BIOGRAPHY, with Ann Charters
I Love: The Story of Vladimir Mayakovsky and Lili Brik

TRANSLATIONS
Baltics (from the Swedish of Tomas Transtromer)
We Women (from the Swedish of Edith Sodergran)
The Courtyard (from the Swedish of Bo Carpelan)

MUSIC
Jazz: New Orleans 1885-1963
The Country Blues
Jazz: A History of the New York Scene
The Poetry of the Blues
The Bluesmen
Robert Johnson
The Legacy of the Blues: Art and Lives of Twelve Great Bluesmen
Sweet as the Showers of Rain
The Swedish Fiddlers
The Roots of the Blues: An African Search

A NOVEL BY SAMUEL CHARTERS

Elvis Presley Calls His Mother
After The Ed Sullivan Show

COFFEE HOUSE PRESS :: MINNEAPOLIS :: 1992

Thanks go to Cowles Media/Star Tribune, Minnesota State Arts Board, and Northwest Area Foundation for support of this project.

Coffee House Press books are available to bookstores through our primary distributor, Consortium Book Sales & Distribution, 287 East Sixth Street, Suite 365, Saint Paul, Minnesota 55101. Our books are also available through all major library distributors and jobbers, and from most small press distributors, including Bookpeople, Bookslinger, Inland, and Small Press Distribution. For personal orders, catalogs, or other information, write to:
Coffee House Press
27 No. Fourth St., Suite 400, Minneapolis, Mn. 55401

Library of Congress Cataloguing-in-Publication Data

Charters, Samuel Barclay.
 Elvis Presley calls his mother after the Ed Sullivan show : a novel / by Samuel Charters.
  p. cm.
 ISBN 0-918273-98-6
 1. Presley, Elvis, 1935-1977--Fiction. 2. Ed Sullivan Show (Television program)--Fiction. I. Title.
 PS3553.H327E45 1992
 813'.54--dc20

                                        92-2573
                                          CIP

9 8 7 6 5 4 3 2 1

For Rococo Kelley —
who would have known what this is all about —
with love.

ARGUMENT

Everything that heard him play,
Even the billows of the sea,
Hung their heads and they lay by.

In sweet music is such art
Killing care and grief of heart
Falling asleep, or hearing die.

> Shakespeare, *Henry VIII*,
> describing Orpheus

I came out on stage, and I was scared stiff. My first big appearance in front of an audience. And I came out and I was doing a fast type tune, one of my first records, and everybody was hollering and I didn't know what they were hollering at. Everybody was screaming and everything and I came off stage and my manager told me they was hollering because I was wiggling. Well, I went back out for an encore and I kind of did a little more. And the more I did, the wilder they went.

> Elvis Presley, describing his appearance at the
> Overton Park Band Shell in Memphis, July 30, 1954

What was he doing, the great god Pan,
Down in the reeds by the river?
Spreading ruin and scattering ban,
Splashing and paddling with the hoofs of a goat,
And breaking the golden lilies afloat
With the dragon-fly on the river.

> Robert Browning

The next thing we know there are gals on stage and they have gone berserk. It looked like they were trying to eat him all up. They were tearing and clawing like animals. Then one of the legs of his pants went. Then his shirt was torn to shreds. It was just scary for me to see what human beings could be driven to. I had always known about the swooning and screaming, but this was incredible. We managed to get him off stage, in shreds.

> Red West, friend and later security for Elvis Presley, describing a concert in Orlando, Florida

And that dismal cry rose slowly
And sank slowly through the air,
Full of spirit's melancholy
And Eternity's despair!
And they heard the words it said —
Pan is dead! great Pan is dead!
Pan, Pan is dead!

> Robert Browning

It was like all the leaves were dying. It was weird . . . like everything died.

> Ginger Alden, who was with Elvis Presley the night of his death, August 15, 1977

Elvis Presley Calls His Mother After The Ed Sullivan Show

Now Momma, you got to understand I didn't have no idea what all those camera people were doing when the show went out over the air. I know Mr. Sullivan had some kind of idea to make people sit up a little by having just the top part of me showing on the screen, but I couldn't tell anything different was happening when I was doing my show. Is that what they did? You couldn't see what I was doing with my legs? You couldn't see anything at all below where I have my guitar hanging when I go out there on stage? I know what you're telling me, but I can't hardly believe that. I think some of the girls that were watching at home, I think those girls are feeling they missed the best part.

Alright, Momma. I won't do it again. But you know I don't mean nothing by it when I say things like that. I'm just talking the way boys out on the road with me and all do. That's the kind of thing they say. When I say something like that I'm just trying to give you a little idea of how those boys carry on. But to do something like that when I'm doing my show! I don't know myself what Mr. Sullivan and everybody else was getting themselves all worked up about. That's the truth. I already did those shows with those other people, Mr. Dorsey and Mr. Allen. You saw me making my appearances on those shows on that television I bought for you all down there. I danced around a little while Scotty was doing his guitar break and I didn't see nobody working themselves up into a sweat over it. I even did this show before. Two times. I know you watched me. And now this time Mr. Sullivan gives these interviews to the newspapers telling them it's too dangerous for people sitting in their living rooms to watch what I'm doing with my legs up on his stage.

I think the truth of it is he was just trying to get people to turn on their TVs to see what was going on. Mr. Sullivan is smart like an old dog, and I think all those newspaper people was just letting on they thought he was being serious and all in what he was telling them. Somebody like him who's in the business of putting on shows will do anything he can to

2

get people to look at what he's presenting. He's always going to tell people that they should look at his next show because that's the one that's going to have something special. The newspaper people know about all that kind of thing because that's the way they do themselves, so they let Mr. Sullivan say anything he wants.

I know for sure that if he was all so worried about me being a menace he didn't have to have me on his show. Where'd I get that word, *menace*? That wasn't anything anybody said on the show here. I saw it in some newspaper. Some of those college kids that don't like what I'm doing have been going around selling buttons that have "I Like Ludwig" printed on them — you know, Beethoven — because they want to stop "The Menace." That's the word they used for me.

No, I didn't do anything no different when I was out on the stage. I didn't do anything that wasn't like I always do when I'm out in front of the public. You know, I just shook myself up a little when I was singing and kind of twisted my legs around. Now that idea Mr. Sullivan had of cutting off the bottom part of me, that was to make people think I was doing something different. You know I never would do anything out there on the stage that wasn't right for people to see. Those shakes I put in is just so the

3

girls will have a little show. Most of the time they all screaming so loud I know they can't hear what I'm singing so I give them something to look at. The people who work on the show told me Mr. Sullivan got a lot of letters sent in after the first show saying what I was doing upset some of the folks out there watching, but that was the most people that ever turned on their TV to watch anything. Forty-four million people! That's more people than I'm ever going to see in my life, and every one of them, they already have seen me!

The truth of it is, when you got that many people looking at you there's always going to be some who don't like what you're doing. The people from Mr. Sullivan's office said that what they got in the letters was the parents writing in to tell them that my kind of dancing wasn't what their children should be looking at. I think that's what give Mr. Sullivan the idea to only put half of me on the screen. He told the newspapers some kind of story like that. I can read you just what he said. "The kids love him and the adults don't, so we shot half of him to please everyone."

Where'd I get that? The publicity people who work for the record company want me to know what they're saying about me in the newspapers so I can be ready for the kinds of things they ask when I do

4

interviews. There's a whole pile of stories cut out of magazines and newspapers and all that in the room here and I'm supposed to look at them when I don't have anything else to do. But you know how it is, they've always got something else they want me to do. If they don't want me to go someplace and get my picture taken, then they want me to meet somebody from some radio station who's been playing my records, or else it's somebody else from some newspaper who wants to write another story. But this time I did get to read some of what they left me.

You not sleepy yet? I can hear it in your voice, Momma. You wide awake like I am. That's why I always call you when I get off a show. I know you're sitting in the house down there in Memphis trying to get yourself tired enough to go to sleep. I know I will be tired in a little while, after everything they put me through to do the show today, but I'm not starting to feel it yet. I'm just like you, Momma. I feel like my head's got something chasing around inside it and I'm not going to get any sleep until it all quiets down in there.

You know, they try to throw away all the clippings that say something bad about me. They don't want me to worry about anything. They just keep telling me all I got to do is sing. But sometimes there's a slip-up and some of the bad stories get mixed in with the others. You wouldn't believe how there's some people out there who really get upset over what I'm doing. I won't read you the things they write because you'd just get yourself all worked up — and you know better anyway. I think whoever is doing the writing over at Time Magazine, that one's the worst one. When the story isn't saying bad things about my singing, it's making fun of the way I eat and the way I talk. No matter what kind of answers I give them when they interview me, they just go ahead and write whatever they want in their story. One place here the fellow just starts off by telling everybody what I ate for lunch. "He was invited to watch Elvis eat a modest lunch, a bowl of gravy, a bowl of mashed potatoes, nine slices of crisp bacon, a quart of milk, a big glass of tomato juice, lettuce salad, six slices of bread, four pats of butter." Now the one that wrote that, I tell you, Momma, I let him come talk to me while I was eating because he said that was the only time he could do the interview. So he writes about what I was eating. What's that got to do with the way I sing?

If I wanted I could write a story of my own about the way those fellows eat. They always start off with two or three drinks, even when they see that I don't have anything to drink myself. Then after they've had something to drink, they order the most expensive thing they can find on the menu, since when they're doing a story somebody else pays for what they're eating. Half of the time they show up with some girl and I never know what she's doing there, only I know she isn't the girl they're married to. Then they always look funny at me when I eat gravy, but that's just the way I grew up, eating the gravy you fixed for me. The things they eat, I couldn't even pronounce the names of half of them.

I know I'm supposed to be friendly with them, and I answer all the questions they ask me over and over. It always the same questions. Over and over. I only wish once that somebody would ask me a question I hadn't heard a hundred times already. But if I look like I'm tired of it, then when the story comes out it says things like I was "pouty" or "sulky." That's the kind of words they use. One of those fellows come along when I was getting my hair cut and he wrote in his article that I was a "sexhibitionist," because I kept looking in the mirror while I was answering his questions. But everybody looks in the mirror when he's getting a haircut. Every time I talk, they write down that I'm "groaning." I think what's happening is that all of them have got something in for people from the South, because a lot of times what they making fun of is the way everybody talks that comes from Mississippi. If I say "I am" they write it down A-H-M. What kind of word is that? If they going to make fun of me why don't they make fun of somebody like that actor, Mr. Laughton. You remember he was the one who took over for Mr. Sullivan when I did the first program. The way Mr. Laughton talks would make people laugh just as much if Time Magazine wrote it down that way. The way he says "I am" would come out something like E-Y-E-M.

But they don't make fun of him because he's a big movie star. I'll tell you something about him, too, Momma. When we did the show you remember I was still out in Hollywood finishing up my picture and he was in the studio doing the announcing. I had to be in the studio out there waiting for the signal to come in. The fellows I was working on the picture with, they said it was a good thing I wasn't back there because he was liable to get all excited with me around. That's right. They said he's that way about men. I don't know anything about it, but that's what they told me. But of course you don't see anything bad about him in the papers because he's such a big star. What I want to know is, when do I get big enough so they'll stop writing these things about me?

No, it's not late here. You can tell by the noise you're hearing over the phone that all the boys are just as wide awake as you and me. I know they going to do some partying before they go off to bed.

They always want to do a little partying when we get through with a show, and that program with Mr. Sullivan was the biggest show going on in America right now. It's the last time I'm going to be working for him. I told you that. He got the Colonel in his office and said he wanted to have me back for three more shows, but the Colonel says that I done so well for him he'd have to pay four hundred thousand dollars to get me back. Mr. Sullivan said that was too much money, so we're not coming back. Maybe that was why he only let people see half of me. There's all those people out there who want to see what I'm doing with my legs, and when he disappoints them like that maybe they won't want to watch me again.

But it's like I said, I just don't know what it is that's got people so worked up. You remember those shows I did with Mr. Dorsey. He had those girls who did those dances. The June Taylor Dancers. I never did anything like they did. They'd come out on the stage with just little bathing suits on, and they'd have feathers on or something fastened on them behind so you'd notice them even more. I think half the shows I been on there's been girls dressed up like that doing some kind of dancing. They don't wear anything on their legs and half the time they go around shaking even more than I do. What would I look like if I came out and did the same thing? Can you imagine what it would be like, Momma? Instead of carrying my guitar I'd come out on the stage wearing my swimming trunks and I'd have some kind of scarf tied around my head and I'd have some kind of thing attached to my behind.

Now if I did that, coming out there plucked like a chicken and going around like those girls do, you know, shaking and putting my behind out — and I'm not making it up, you've seen them — if I did that then you know what would happen. I think the President would call up and tell the Army to come stop the show. But if the girls do it, it's all right. Everybody on the show smiles and the audience claps and some of the men whistle at the girls' legs, but nobody thinks anything about it. But if I do it, people act like I'm some old man showing himself under a raincoat when he walks down the street.

I know what you're saying. That's just the kind of world we're living in and I shouldn't take it personal. But I've been doing that kind of dancing ever since I started making records. You remember how I did those same kinds of things with my legs when I played on that country show in Memphis way back at the beginning. When I come off the stage some of the other boys singing on the show got hot with me over what I was doing. They called me some names because they had to go out on the stage after I had left the audience feeling a little wild. You know what one of the boys in Mr. Sullivan's orchestra said to me tonight, Momma? He told me, Mr. Sullivan's planning to cut you off in the middle tonight on account of you just going to do the same old thing you done before and he's going to try to make it look like you doing something new. And even if it wasn't new, why would I want to do something different? I got where I am by doing things the same way. I don't see why I should go changing now.

But it looked like I was doing something special? You mean some people thought it was all just some new act I was putting on? I'd like to see the faces of some of those people back in Memphis when they read about how dangerous I've become all of a sudden. If I just stand there and shake my legs around a little then the whole country's going to come to a stop. I guess if you look at it one way that's Mr. Sullivan's talent. It's like I said. He gives people the idea that something special's going to happen. But if people do stop and look at what I'm doing, you know why that is. You and me both know the truth about that. It's all happening because I'm using what God gave me to use. That's what it's all about. I wouldn't be where I am if I was trying to do it all by myself.

Just a minute, Momma, I got to put the phone down.

Can't you all shut up in there? I can't hear myself talking and I got my mother on the phone. You know Momma wants to know what I'm doing, and if you carrying on like that she's going to get the idea we're having a party.

How do you do, miss. Which one of the boys sent you in to see me? He was the one? Well, let me tell you he does know how to pick out a pretty one. I'm not going to be long on the telephone here, so you just find yourself some place to sit down and wait for me. I tell you what, you go over there on one of the beds. That way you won't have to move or nothing. One of the boys is going to be bringing in something so you can get yourself a Coke. You can get me a Coke at the same time. If you hungry I know we got some cheeseburgers coming up in a little while. You just ask if there's anything you want around here. I know we're going to have a good time, just you and me.

Momma, can you hear me alright now? You know how it gets when we finish one of these shows. There's all kind of business to talk over, and just like I said, the boys get together and throw a party for themselves. That's the way they do every time,

and it's no different just because it's New York.
New York? That's right, you never been up here,
but it isn't anything so very special, and the way
they do things doesn't feel right to me. All these
agents and show people, they try to get you to make
up your mind in one minute. It's like they all want
to go and do something else, and if you want to
think about what they're telling you then you getting in their way.

If I only learned one thing growing up the way we
did, you and me and Daddy Vernon, it was that I
have to do things my own way. If it takes me two
minutes to make up my mind about something, or if
it takes me two hours, then that's what it takes.
These men up here, they think because they have
these big offices with their names on the doors and
pictures on the walls of lots of famous people, they
think they know what's going on in music now.
What they don't understand is that I'm changing
everything in their kind of music business, and it's
all going to be different when I get through. Wait a
minute —

*You all going to have to keep it quiet in there or I'm
going to put every one of you out on the street. Oh
no, honey, don't you get up. I wasn't talking about
you. It's just those guys in the other room. Sometimes they forget how they're supposed to act when*

13

they get indoors. They been driving up and down the highways so long they think they can act like some kind of truck drivers. You hear me, what I'm saying, in there? If you want to look at something, honey, there's all those things out of the newspapers they leave around for me to look at. Sometimes they get pretty funny, and sometimes it doesn't seem to me that they're funny at all.

Momma, you said you got a lot of letters from this girl who says she and I have a very serious relationship with each other. I can tell you all about that "serious relationship" she says we've been having. I have to face the facts about the life I been leading, and anybody who has come up before the public the way I have, his life isn't private any more. I know that, and that's the way it's going to be, but that girl who's writing you, I couldn't even tell you what she looks like. I know she says I told her this or I told her that, but she never looked the same way twice, and I couldn't tell you which way she had of looking was how she really looked. That girl was really crazy to get to meet us. It wasn't just me she wanted to meet, Momma. You know how those girls are. I don't even remember which city it was where she started hanging around us. Her name was Evie, or Ivy, something like that. She says it's Evaline? That could be it. The first time I met this Evie — if that's who she is — she was with one of those people from a radio station where I was doing an interview. It was a woman who was doing the interviewing, and this Evie was a friend of hers and she said she just had come along for company.

I suppose she does look really pretty in the picture she sent you. I remember she didn't look so bad, but we always see pretty girls everyplace we go. So this Evie or Ivy, she didn't have much to say at the interview. She just kind of hung around on the side listening to what was going on, you know, the answers I was giving. She had long hair, and she had on a sweater and slacks that night. I kind of noticed what she was doing because she was really listening to what I was telling this friend of hers. Most of the time when people are talking to me they don't listen to anything I tell them, even when I'm trying to answer the questions they ask me. They write down what I say, but they don't hear it. All they're doing is seeing how I look up close. It's like they're trying to decide if what Mr. Sullivan says is true, that I'm too dangerous to have around the house. No, that's the truth, and I have to accept that fact. There is some people who think that way about what I'm doing.

But this girl was listening to what I was saying. She had her long hair all teased up, and you know I always look twice at a girl who's got her hair fixed like that, but what I was noticing was that she was listening with her face very serious, and when I said something she agreed with she would give a little nod. Then after the interview was finished she waited until her friend had gone away, then she looked at me in a funny way and she asked me if I was famous. I said I was known in certain sections, but I wasn't known everywhere. "That's famous enough," is what she said next. "I never have known anybody who was famous. Do you feel any different from me?"

She asked me that and I started laughing and I said, "Ma'am, how do you feel? Unless you can give me some little idea, I can't tell you if I'm any different."

So she looked all around the room, and she told me, "Maybe I know some things you don't know. I know why that window's there, and I know the names of the flowers on the curtain, and I know where you go if you walk through the door there and walk up the stairs. Does that make me different from you?"

I wouldn't have hung around talking to her except that the boys had already got everything out of the cars and put it up in the hotel room, so there wasn't nothing for me to do once I was through with the interview. I told her I didn't know any of those things, so it didn't make no difference if I was famous or not.

She was quiet for a little, then she pushed her hair back a little, being real careful not to get it tangled, and she started laughing too. "That sounds like I take myself very seriously when I tell you I'm different from you. I don't mean I'm anybody important. I'm not at all. But everybody is different from anybody else in some little way. That's all I meant."And when she said that, she put her head to one side and she looked at me for a while. "There is something about you," she said, "and I don't mean that you have nice eyes or that you comb your hair in a special way. I can see it most whenever you move. Just now you turned a little bit. There. That's what I meant. You did it because you thought you'd look a little better if you were turned around part way, and you know I'm looking at you." And she pushed her hair back again. "You don't even know who I am, but here you're doing these things, making these little movements, because you know I'm looking at you."

"What I wonder about" — she still was talking — "is if you moved around like that before you got famous, or if that's one of the things that made you get famous. What's that mean anyway, to be famous? Oh, I don't want to sound like my friend. I'm not interviewing you for some newspaper. I just want to know what you think." So I told her that being famous meant that people knew who you were. She

17

thought about that, then she wrinkled up her nose at me. "That's not good enough. They might know *who* you are, but at the same time they won't stop worrying about it until they know *what* you are, and I can see that could get hard sometimes."

That was her way of talking, Momma, and she said she had to go after that and I didn't think I'd see her again. But then she turned up again later on. She must have known somebody at the hotel where we were staying, because they weren't supposed to let any people come up, but she still was around when I sent down for room service to bring me up something to eat. When I heard a knocking on the door I went to open it up and there she was, holding a tray in her hands and she had a napkin over her arm, just like you see those waiters in the movies. Evie, or Ivy, just sat down at the end of the bed with her knees pulled up and she watched me eat. You know I had had so many people watching me after all that's happened, so I don't pay no attention to it. And that was just what she said. "You don't care if I watch you or don't watch you when you're thinking about what you're eating. Then you think about me being here and you do something like rubbing your hand along the side of your face, just like you did a minute ago, so I'll see you doing it and I'll pay attention to you. And I don't mean to make you embarrassed about it, because you're not doing it just for me. You'd do it for anybody. Did you know that?"

I didn't know what she wanted, Momma, and I still don't know, but she stopped talking and leaned back on the cushion so she was looking up at the ceiling. "Before I was sixteen I didn't think any boy would want to have anything to do with me." Now I know what that sounds like, like she was leading up to something, and I thought she wanted me to say something about how pretty she was, but she didn't want to hear that. "No, no, no," she said, "I didn't mean that like I was trying to get you to say something. That's only what's natural. I don't know of a girl who didn't have thoughts just like that. But then you get to be sixteen or seventeen or eighteen, some time around there, and before you notice it, everybody you meet wants to do something with you. Most of the time it's just one thing they want to do, but you know you can be sure about it. They want to make love to you."

Now I know what this all sounds like, but I'm telling you about what she did so you'll know about those letters. After she said that, she looked at me and she said, "But you're not like that. What you want is for me to make love to you. I never met a boy who thought like that," she told me, and then she got up and made a face. "I want to go and think about that," was what she said, and then she went off.

Now I know you getting some idea about her and me, but it wasn't that way. It was strange, was what it was. She stayed around for a couple of weeks then, and that was the time I said I never did see her look the same way twice. We always gave orders to keep people out of the hotels and the backstages in those theaters because it gets so crowded in there I don't know whether I'm coming or going sometimes, and what I'm supposed to be doing is getting out on that stage. But she could find her way in, no matter what anybody said to her. The next day, when I wasn't thinking about anything, I saw somebody putting the flowers in the dressing room and this person with the flowers had on one of those uniforms with baggy pants, like those messengers have, and she turned around and there she was. She waved around the room at all the flowers people had sent and she looked kind of confused. She shrugged her shoulders a little and she sat down.

"Maybe I'm just like the girls sending you all these flowers," she said to me. "Maybe I'm just like them and I don't know it. Do you think I'm like them?"

And I said, "No, ma'am, I don't think I've met anybody like you before." She had put her hair up to keep it under the cap that came with her uniform, but she took the cap off and she looked so funny in that dumb uniform with that long hair falling down that I couldn't help laughing a little, and she didn't know what to do.

"Do you know what?" she asked me when I had stopped laughing. "I bought a ticket to hear you sing tonight. I never have gone to one of these shows before."

I told her there was so much noise she never was going to hear me sing. If that's what she wanted she should go out and buy her one of my records, but she said no, if there was all that noise and scream-ing that was part of it and she wanted to hear that too. What she was trying to find out was who I was, or who somebody like me was, and she wouldn't find out anything until she could see who the audi-ence was that I was doing it all for.

No, it isn't late, Momma. You know we don't get to sleep when we've finished with a show. When I have you to talk to I don't sleep anyway. Don't we always talk like this when I can't sleep and I know you're back there at home feeling just as awake as I am? We've always been doing it just this way, and that's one thing that don't ever change.

That girl? I didn't see her for a day or two. We had already gone five hundred miles and I didn't think she could catch up to us, but she borrowed a maid's

ELVIS PRESLEY CALLS HIS MOTHER

uniform at the hotel we were staying at and she came into my room with a bucket and a mop and a pile of towels. She had her hair all tucked up again, but this time it was under one of those maid's caps. She laid the towels on the dresser and she put the bucket down on the floor and she sat down on the bed like she did the first night when we talked. "I liked your singing," was the first thing she said. "What you said was right, I couldn't hear much of it, but what I could hear, I liked. It got everybody excited around me."

"How about you?" I asked her.

"I could feel something. I was watching all the things you were doing, and I could see why you were doing them, to get those girls all worked up. I could feel it, but it wasn't any different from being in the room with you. You do the same things when it's just one person you're with. The only difference is you work harder on the stage, because you want to make sure nobody misses what you're doing. Did you know that?"

"No," I said. "I never did think anything about it."

"I don't think you ever did." She was kind of thoughtful about the things she was telling me, and I tell you the truth, I never did have anybody tell me things about myself the way she did.

"Let me tell you one thing I know about you now. If you didn't always do that, if you didn't do those things when you're just in a room here with somebody like me, you know, all those things you do when you move and hold yourself, then you couldn't do it for all those thousands of people out there in the theater. That music you do, you know it's kind of simple. Did you know *that?*"

Now nobody had ever asked me that question and I just looked at her, surprised. "It's so simple it's almost like it isn't there. It's like somebody was thinking of a song and they just put down some little ideas to get them started. Like an outline. Then what you do, you come out there and you fill in all those empty lines, and what you fill them up with is you. I liked that. I learned something about you from that."

After that she started to hang the towels up in the bathroom, and I know it sounds crazy, but she started in mopping the floor. I was beginning to wonder who she was and I asked her if she didn't have a job or something, and she told me she had left things kind of behind for a little while. She had a job and she was going to have to go back to it, but she had to find out some things first. She said there was some fellow who wanted to marry her and she didn't want to decide anything just yet. I could tell her all about that, because I have the same feelings when it comes to getting married.

But why is she writing you those letters? Well, Momma, we had some trouble. She showed up three or four more times, always in some kind of clothes she had borrowed so she could get in to see me. Then the last time she came around looking just like all the others girls who come to see the shows. You know, with her hair all fixed and with a little skirt and a sweater that didn't fit her, and I said, "What you doing this time?" And she said, "I think I'm learning to be like you."

Then the next morning I went around to the rooms to get everybody on the road again, and there she was, in bed with one of the guys. I looked at her very hard, and she sat up with just a sheet around her and she shook her head and she looked kind of sad the way I did. Finally she said, "You were an ocean I would have drowned in. I needed to have some little calmer place where I could get my feet wet. You know I said you wanted me to make love to you. I couldn't do what you wanted."

I stood there looking at her and I got madder and madder and right then and there I made her get out of the hotel. I told her we didn't let anybody stay around once we got started out driving, and she had to get out of there before I called down to the desk and had somebody take her out. Her eyes got very big and I thought she was going to cry, but she didn't say anything again. She just waited until I was gone from the room, then she got her things and she left. I had thought all the time she was different, and she really was trying to find out why I was so different from other people, but instead she does something like that and says funny things to try to make up for it. So it don't matter to me what she says in those letters. And don't you think about it again.

Will you all get out of here? Every damn one of you. I'm trying to talk on the phone and I got no time to mess with your party. Man, what you doing with that bedspread wrapped all around your legs?

Momma, you know how crazy the boys are sometimes. Well, right now they got some of their girlfriends in here and they're having a contest to see which one of them looks the most like me. That bedspread he's got on—you know, all dark-colored—that's one of the boys imitating the lower half of me cut off on the TV screen, just the way Mr. Sullivan did on the show. But he's not doing it so good. He'd not doing it any good at all. I don't like to say it, but what he's doing looks more like a hula dance than anything else.

Well, no, I don't mean to say the hula dance isn't pretty, and I know a girl like you could do it better than I could, but this is my dancing you all are talking about, and he hasn't got it a bit. Even after all the times he's stood backstage watching me do it.

Look out. Now did you see that? Or did I do it too fast for you? That's what you got to do with your hips. I'm going to do it again, so you can see what I'm doing.

Now you all are going to have to quiet down and I don't want no more screaming. You hear me! What do you think you're doing now? You get that bedspread wrapped around you again. I don't go along with that kind of thing. You get out, you hear what I'm telling you? You all just get out!

I hope you weren't listening to all that. It got kind of crazy there for a minute. The boys were pretending to be me and some of the girls were singing a little to help out. They were doing a little of that kind of twisting I do with my legs, and the one that had the bedspread wrapped around him so he'd look like I did on the show, he let the bedspread drop down on the floor and he didn't have anything on underneath it but his jockey shorts. The noise you heard was all the girls squealing. Yes, Momma, all of them were in the room at the same time. They were the kind of girls the boys bring along. I was calling them all ladies, but they really wasn't ladies at all. They didn't see anything they didn't know about.

You know that doesn't have anything to do with me, and now they've gone off to do their partying in the other rooms. But wouldn't you know, when they were going out they took all the food with them. You wait a minute while I get myself something to eat, then we can go on talking.

I don't know about these guys I travel around with. They took all the cheeseburgers, and what they did leave me was cold already. It gets to be crazy sometimes, even when I'm trying to keep everybody thinking about what they should be doing. When I was coming back down the hallway from the bathroom, I looked in one of the rooms, and there was some of those people who write those articles about us sitting in a corner, and they were looking at everything that was going on with their eyes as wide open as a cat trying to see in the dark. They weren't writing anything down, but I could see they were catching all of it.

I know I'll see some kind of thing in some magazine when they do write something about the little party the boys are having. But they never get it right. They always think everything we do is so serious.

What they put down in their story is always something about how we always have us a party because we have so much pressure on us when we go out on the stage and everything. Nobody ever says we do it because we're mostly a bunch of kids and we just like to party.

Okay, I know you're right about that, I'm twenty-one years old, and I shouldn't think of myself as a kid, but some of the guys that carry stuff up on the stage for us and make sure people don't come and bother us when we're trying to get some sleep— they're just eighteen or nineteen. They don't have no sense at all. You know I have a little sense. You give it to me. That's how I got enough sense to know what's going on here.

But that's what's wrong with everything they're saying about rock and roll. When they write those articles and they put out those fan magazines, they don't understand that half of the things we're doing is just to have us some fun. If people didn't get so worried and they stopped looking so hard at what I'm doing with my legs, they could see that most of the time I'm laughing at it myself. That's what rock and roll is all about. It's just guys like me having fun for the kids. Now when I sing a ballad, that's different. I'm saying something else to the people out there. But I don't get to sing so many ballads because that doesn't seem to be what people are looking for from me, but you know I always liked to sing all kinds of songs. With rock and roll, everybody's always asking me how long it's going to last, and if it isn't going to be around for such a long time we might as well have a little fun with it.

Those things we do on the stage now, even when the colored people did them at the beginning they didn't pretend like it was all serious. They was just having themselves some fun. I know sometimes I pretend to be serious, with all that dancing and those things I do on the stage, but if I didn't laugh at it a little bit people would think I was crazy.

Oh, I know, people get worked up at the dancing and all those songs saying I'd like to make love to girls. I forget when I'm up there singing that anybody who gives people ideas about making love and things like that is going to get in trouble. But that's what they're thinking about anyway. When I shake a little bit it just makes them think about what's already in their minds. As long as the singing is all pretty and nice, like Perry Como and Bing Crosby, then nobody gets upset. It's like they have a secret little game they play with the kids out in the audience. They won't sing about what's really on the kids' minds and the audience gives them all kinds of applause for keeping their secret. Now

Perry Como, he'll suggest a little something in some of his songs, but that's just to remind everybody of all the things he's not saying. You don't think that's what's going on? I know it's something like that or I wouldn't have so many people getting all worried about what I'm doing — like Mr. Sullivan cutting my legs off when he's putting his show out over the air.

What I'm showing everybody up on the stage is that those boys out there in the audience want to do a lot more than just kiss those girls. And when the girls start screaming like that, they're letting everybody know that they know what those boys are thinking about. So I'm telling everybody's secrets. But you won't tell any of my secrets, will you, Momma?

I think if any of those people who say they're critics could come out on the stage with us they'd stop writing some of those things about how serious it is singing rock and roll. Like I told that girl who was writing you those letters, with all the screaming that's going on we can't hardly hear what we're doing. It gets real frustrating for Scotty sometimes, because he's trying to play his break on the guitar and I'm jumping around a little and the noise just comes right over the front of the stage and I feel sometimes like all that noise is going to climb on top of us if I don't do something to push it back. Of course, what Bill's playing on the bass, me and Scotty's the only ones that can tell what note he's playing anyway, so if he just wanted to run up and down the scale nobody would notice. I used to get scared out there because of all the noise. If those kids meant all those things they shouting then I'd never get out of there with my clothes on.

If those writers could just come out there with me one time— It isn't just the noise. You know, Momma, half the time we can't see anything with all those lights shining in our eyes. I can see about as far as the edge of the stage, because the light hits that much, but once you get past that I can't hardly see if there's people standing up or sitting down or whatever they're doing. When we first started going around it wasn't so bad because the lights weren't so strong, but now I've come to be so big and so many people wanting to see me, those lights get so bright out there I sometimes think they're going to burn me up.

I'll tell you something, and if somebody says anything to you about how I'm a menace on account of my dancing you just tell them about this. We came out in a theater on our way to New York, and I could see the master of ceremonies introducing us and I came out and started to sing, but I didn't feel we were getting the hand we should have had. There was shouting and all, but it didn't seem to be as loud as it should be. I sang "Heartbreak" and "Hound Dog" and "Don't Be Cruel," just like always, but because I was trying to go over big I started to let it all out when I was dancing around with the microphone the way I do. Then I thought, I'm going to really give this audience something to remember Elvis Presley with, and without telling Scotty or Bill what I was going to do I just went up to the edge of the stage and jumped down into the audience.

So I was standing there waiting for the girls to start screaming, but when I looked around I was all by myself. The reason we couldn't hear so much from the stage was that the police had moved everybody. back from the front rows of the auditorium so they wouldn't get so excited. All I could see was about twenty empty rows of seats and then a whole lot of policemen's backs. It all had happened so fast that there wasn't no spotlight on me, so I was just in the dark. I was standing there waiting to have everybody jump all over me, but after a minute the girls in the audience decided I was all finished and they started getting angry because they thought they were getting cheated by the show being so short. Of course, Bill and Scotty just kept going, because they knew that when I did jump around like that I usually would come back in on the same number. But I didn't want to come crawling back up on the stage again, because that would give people the idea of the dumb thing I'd done, so I looked for a door so I could go around the back and come out on the stage again like it was all planned.

But it was so dark down there in those empty seats, nobody could see anything. I nearly tripped over myself, but I got to a door down front, and I tried to pull it open. While I was doing that two police came running over and they took hold of my arms and they started to drag me off. "You can't go in there, boy. What do you think you're doing?" All that kind of stuff they were saying. I was trying to make them stop and I kept saying, "Hey man, hey man, I'm Elvis and I got to get me back up on that stage." Finally one of them sees who I am and he starts laughing and I start laughing, and the three of us are standing down there in row one listening to all those girls screaming for me, and there I am in the dark and I can't do anything about it. What they did was take me to the edge of the stage where they knew about some steps, and they give me a push and I jumped out in the spotlight again, waving like I was just coming back because of all the applause. Then I looked at Scott and Bill and D. J. hitting those drums and Bill had gone into one of his comedy routines, hopping up and down with the bass, and they were so gone, those cats were so gone I couldn't keep from laughing again, and then when I got to the microphone and started to sing, I couldn't remember what song it was we were doing. I tell you, that's what happened. And all the time the girls were screaming and screaming and they didn't notice what was happening except I wasn't out there for a minute. If those people who write about us could see something like that they wouldn't take it all so serious.

I got to see if I can find something more to eat. I told them to send downstairs for some more cheeseburgers. You got something there to eat yourself? Don't worry about what it's going to cost me to talk to you. The RCA people take care of everything like that. All I have to do is tell Colonel Parker and he gets it taken off the bill. Anyway, Momma, I don't look at the bills anymore. I got somebody else to take care of all that. I know this rock and roll won't go on for long, but I don't worry. If it loses out I can always do some other kind of singing. I don't worry about anything. Would you, Momma, if it was you doing the singing and everything was going so good?

You know I just come by the room where those writers were sitting a while ago and they're still all there and I don't think any of them have smiled about anything. They're talking to one of the guys that's working with us, and he's heard me interviewed so many times he's giving them all my answers. All that stuff about the colored people doing the same kind of show only nobody noticed it until some white cat come along and started doing it their way. I stood outside listening to them, keeping myself out of the way so they wouldn't notice, and this guy even stood up and started to show them about the dancing I do, showing them how I goosed up what the colored people had been doing and that's why everybody's noticing it now.

I don't want to talk about those writers so much, but they did say some pretty mean things about me in the papers and the magazines. I think another thing they got wrong is trying to use words to tell about what I'm doing. They think I have everything all decided and I've worked out what I'm doing and when I go out on the stage I have some kind of plan to show people what I'm thinking. That isn't the way it goes with my kind of music. I just go out there and go crazy. If there were any words for what I was doing, I'd just stand there like Mr. Como and sing the words. But even if I could think up any words they wouldn't let me sing them on the stage anyway. That's what gets those writers all mixed up. They're trying to use words to describe something that there isn't words to describe. That doesn't work when they're writing about anybody, and I think that's the cause of so much writing being so bad when it applies to me, or when it applies to anything when it comes out of someplace except your head. I'm just using a new way to show something, and they're still trying to write about in the same old way.

Just a minute, Momma. Why don't you go get yourself a Coke and put a little something in it and then you come on back.

Man, what you doing in here? I'm pleased to meet you lady, but what did you bring her in here for? Man, no, you got to be crazy. You can't do it right there in the bed. I'm talking on the telephone to my mother and what would she say if she heard you grunting in the background there. Lady, I think you've had too much to drink. I think both of you have had too much to drink. Lady, don't you have anything on under that blanket? No, you sure don't. What did you do, get started in the other room and you got chased out? Come on, get up off the bed. I told you it has to be someplace else. I don't care if somebody's getting something in every bed in the place. Lady, you dropped all those things you were carrying and I don't want them lying there on my floor. I have a very nice young lady coming back to visit me and she wouldn't want to see things messed up.

What's that thing in your hand? It's one of those little rubber girdles? I don't know why you girls put on those things when you come to party. You know you just going to take them off. Come on, get up off the bed, stop doing that. Man, if you so ready to get it off just find a place on the floor somewhere. I know the floor isn't all filled up. But just get out of here. I got my mother on the phone and she's going to be back in a minute. Take that girdle with you. Come on now, baby, nobody's saying anything against a little rocking and rolling. You just got to find yourselves someplace else to do it in. And if you see that girl who was here with me, tell her I'll be off the telephone soon and then she and I can get to know each other a little better. And when you talking to her try to keep yourself covered up. I don't want her to get any wrong ideas about the kind of parties we have here.

Momma, did you get yourself something to drink? I know. I know. It's getting late and they going to get me up just like always to do some crazy interview first thing in the morning, but you know I don't sleep the way I should. I do a show like that and it really wears me out so that I have to eat a little, and that gets me all waked up and then I have to start again to get ready to sleep. Somebody looked at me tonight and said, man, you got it made, doing what you want anytime you get ready, but I really feel like a yo-yo, just going up and down. I get all wound up with some sleep and some rest when I'm traveling, then I let it all out when I'm singing and I got to come back up the string, a little bit at a time, and sometimes I can feel my arms getting tired when I pull myself up.

I was telling you about how the lights get so bright up there on the stage I sometimes can't see so good out in the theater. There was one time, Momma, before Colonel Parker started taking care of business for me, when Bill and Scotty and me got hired to play for a private party. I think it was down in Alabama someplace. We were going to play one of those shows in Louisiana—you know that Hay Ride Show we did—and we thought we could swing past this little town and do the job and get a little extra money.

It was one of those kind of places with lots of bright lights shining right in our eyes and we couldn't make out anything except that everybody seemed to have some kind of costume on. Okay, we said, it's going to be a costume party, and we can go out and do our show, just like always. We didn't let the crowd bother us none in those kind of places. Even with all the lights shining I could see people kind of crowding to get close when we started and I thought everything was going to be alright. But they didn't make much noise, even when I shook it up a little for them, and I figured, well, they got those costumes on and that must keep them dampered down a little. But when we finished the number and I went into my bow, there wasn't any kind of sound out of them. Everything was so quiet you couldn't tell they were breathing. Finally somebody said something in a loud voice right down in front. What he said was, "Boy, can't you do nothing but that nigger shit?"

Now the fellow that had hired us, he was standing off on the side of the stage, and when he heard that he jumped out there and he started in on the guy that said it. "You told me to get you something really hot, something that's really happening, and this is the boy out of Memphis who's got those records playing everywhere you go. This is Elvis Presley." And the other guy, who's still standing out there in the dark and we can't really get a look at him, he says, "What kind of a name is Elvis?" Then the fellow on the stage with us got upset and he started saying things and he was getting more and more answers from down in front, and finally, to calm everybody down, some of the public crawled up on the stage to get between them. We were still standing there, holding our instruments, and Bill had taken a couple of steps back so he could start running if the trouble got any worse, and then we got a look at their costumes. They were wearing sheets, and they had hoods that they'd pushed back so they could talk. They were white sheets they had on them. It was the Ku Klux Klan. That crazy guy had hired us to play a party for the Ku Klux Klan!

When we saw that, we started to go off the stage, but then the crowd started shouting and whistling. They'd paid their money to see the show and we were the only show they had. The guy down in front was a little quieter and the fellow that had hired us kind of backed up across the stage, coming toward us. He was smiling and waving his arm for everybody to be quiet, but when he got back close to us we could see him shaking. In that part of the country you don't mess around with the Klan. He stood there beside me waving his arms and he whispered out of the side of his mouth, "You know any other kind of numbers?"

We were just about as scared as he was, but when he said that we started in to some hillbilly number. I can't remember what it was. Something you and Daddy Vernon used to sing, and it was so simple we

didn't have to rehearse it. This got everybody qui-
eted down and we sang them every hillbilly number we could think of, but I could see we weren't
going over. You know how I feel when I can't move
around while I'm singing, and I didn't dare do anything that might get them started on us again. Finally I looked over at the guy at the edge of the stage
and he gave us the sign that we'd been out there
singing long enough to get our money.

Now you know I still didn't know what to expect
when we did a show in those days, and I thought
the way to end it was to try to get everybody on my
side. What I did was start singing "The Star-Span-
gled Banner." I figures this would show them that
we were good people, even if we did make a mistake with our first number. But right in the middle
of it the noise started in again and I could see some
of those boys in those white sheets starting to climb
up on the stage again. Bill had more experience
with this kind of show than I did, and when I
stopped playing my guitar and turned around to
ask the guys what I should do, Bill all of a sudden
dragged his bass up to the microphone and started
singing "Dixie" as loud as he could. When they
heard this the boys climbing up on the stage started
walking up and down like it was some kind of
parade and we played "Dixie" over and over for
them until we could get out of there.

41

That isn't the kind of thing that happens to me now, but I still don't know who's out there in the dark half of the time when I'm singing.

Just a minute, Momma. There's somebody who's just come in that I have to say hello to.

Where did you go off to, baby? When I told those girls to get out I wasn't thinking of you. I could tell by looking at them they weren't nice girls. You're different. You just sit down on the bed again and I'll be through talking to my mother and you and me will have all the time we want. Where do you go to school? You don't go to school anymore? You got some kind of job? You sell jewelry at Woolworth's? Woolworth's is a good place to be. One of those big companies you know they won't go out of business on you. Before I was doing this I had a job driving a truck. If nobody likes my movie and people get tired of rock and roll, I can always get my old job back.

I bet you have every one of my records. Well, if you don't have all the new ones you don't need to buy them. Before you leave I'll have one of the boys find all he can for you. But you're not thinking of leaving now. I wouldn't want to think about you going away just before we getting started. I can see you got on a fancy petticoat under that skirt you're wearing. I see the little edge of it there, and it gets me wondering what you got on under that petticoat.

But you stay over on the bed there. I'll just lie back and look at you while I finish talking.

No, Momma, we didn't get cut off. I had my hand over the phone so you wouldn't have to listen to all those business things we have to talk about. No, you don't need to hang up. I can keep talking. I know you're just like me. It's as hard for you to get to sleep as it is for me. You taking your pill? I don't like to take too many pills. Oh, I take them if I have to sleep real bad. I hate it when I lie there and I don't feel like sleeping and I'm too tired to get out of bed and do something else. When I stay up so late it isn't so bad. If it gets to be nine or ten o'clock in the morning then I can sleep.

I had to use the pills when I was out in Hollywood. I had to get up early so I could go to work on the picture. That was the way they did it out there. If I was going to get up and not look like I was a hundred years old, then I had to get to sleep on time. But I don't like to use them. You take yours now, and I'll keep talking until you feel like you want to lie down. It isn't my place to ever say anything about how God made the world, but sometimes I wish He'd made it just a little bit easier to sleep.

Just a minute, Momma.

Miss, if you like everybody else around this crazy place you probably feeling tired. You're not? Honey, I know why that is. You're thinking about what's coming next. You just keep lying there and let me look at those pretty legs of yours.

No, Momma, we didn't get cut off this time either. I just had something to discuss with the boys. You know, like you told me to do, I always have Gene or Junior sleeping in the room with me in case I start to walking around in my sleep, and I had to tell them to wait a little. I wouldn't let them cut off the connection while you still are waiting to get to sleep. Anyway, I know I won't walk off anywhere in my sleep tonight. After all that dancing they had me do in those rehearsals — and then after I got all ready they didn't show it anyway! You know how those people are. I'm telling you the truth, just like the preacher tells the congregation when he wants to let them know they're hearing the word. Listen to this, Momma, What you are hearing is the truth, it's God's truth, it's the one hundred and ten percent truth — and the truth is, when I get into my bed tonight, I'm going to stay right in it and not get up for one minute. And you know I mean every word I'm saying.

Who am I talking to? I'm just talking to you, Momma. And one of the boys—he's still here. Somebody's always watching me so I don't get in any trouble.

Now you're going to keep the promise you made me, aren't you. You and Daddy Vernon are going to come out to Hollywood with me when I start working on my next picture. That's not going to be long. Another three or four weeks and you going to have to get everything ready. And you promised me you would get yourself all the clothes you need to come out there and meet everybody. I know you never had nothing, but I know my Momma. Once you go into one of those stores and begin looking over the clothes they have there you going to come out the best-dressed lady in Memphis, and when you get off that train in Los Angeles you going to have all those reporters asking each other, Who is she? She must be going to do something out here. But we'll put you in a limousine to come out to the studio and that will get them wondering even more. I know there was people used to laugh. They thought there was something funny about us. But they don't laugh no more. Not when they see that it's my Momma coming in the room.

I'm going to tell you a secret. Something just for you and me. I'm going to see to it that you make a screen test too. Yes. Of course you going to do it. They won't ask you to sing. They didn't ask me to sing. You remember me telling about that fellow that done the interview with me. I told him they just had me do a dramatic screen test and I didn't think much about the idea of singing in the movies. That was Charlie Walker in San Antonio. What I said to him was I took strictly an acting test and I wouldn't care too much about singing in the movie since I do enough singing when I'm traveling round. But people all the time were asking me about whether I was going to sing and I told them, no, I'm not, you know.

What they didn't tell me was that they already knew all about my singing. They just wanted to see if I could carry a "dramatic story line" — did you hear how I said that? With that Hollywood way of talking? That's what they call "acting" out here, when you can do all kinds of things with your voice. Bing Crosby and them, they always sing in their movies and they get a good salary for doing it, so I wasn't going to say no when they told me how they wanted it. You know the Colonel. If there's money hiding there someplace he's going to be the one that finds it. So I did whatever they wanted me to do. So now after the picture was such a big success they can do what I want them to do, and what I want is for my mother to do a screen test.

You stop laughing, Momma. You going to get yourself all worked up and then you'll have to go and take another pill and you won't sleep anyway. I'm really serious about you taking a screen test because I want you to be in my next picture. I'll just tell them that there's this lady I discovered — just the way them talent scouts do it — and I want them to see how she can act. I'm not even going to say it's you, Momma. Then when they start in to write the script I'm going to say to them that I'm going to sing a duet with the new singing discovery I found. I'm not afraid to do that. I know everybody's going to say that this new lady sings better than I do, but I'm not afraid about that because I'll know who it is. And that's the truth. When we start in singing one of those gospel numbers you taught to me, you can sing circles all around me. Standing there beside you I feel just like I'm a little kid again.

I know there's not going to be any trouble with you getting a part. The trouble's going to come when they write the story. How they going to come up with a story where a boy can go off and do all the

47

fighting and everything and go into the city and all the things they make me do, and the boy's just thinking about what his mother would think of him?

That's right. He can take her picture out and look at it. You know how they do it. You been to as many pictures as I have. I think if you come to add them all up, you must have been to more than me. But I got this idea. How about a story where the boy has to hide out or something on account of people think he's done something wrong? I got it now. Too bad I don't have somebody to write it down. It'll start out with this boy who's coming back late at night after seeing his girl, and at the same time somebody else driving a car that looks like his runs it off the road and kills an old man that's walking along. Now the boy can't say anything because this girl's momma and daddy won't let him come around to the house. So when everybody starts to say he's the one who done it, he can't say nothing and he gets ready to run off.

Now here's your part. I can see all this just like the movie's going around in my head. You all poor and you living in a little place, something like that court we lived in when we first come to Memphis, and you work in some job because you're a widow. That's how we'll do it this time, then in the next picture we'll have Daddy Vernon come along and marry you! Now this time, you know that your boy wouldn't lie about anything like that, so you talk back to people who say I was the one who was driving the car. And that makes everybody sore at you, just like they sore at me. So we have to run away together.

You like that now? You and me running away together. And the way we'll work the gospel songs into it, when we're running away we have to get off the road and there's one of those gospel tents. When they call for anybody who wants to testify then we can stand up and hold hands and we can sing one of those songs we know. Everybody thinks we can sing real good and they don't care what we're running away from just so we're for Jesus, so we go along with them. After a while we get to be so popular that they let me make little sermons and you play the piano for us when we sing. Of course there's got to be some other things in it — we'll have to work in some girl who wants to take me away from Jesus and turn my thoughts to sin.

Of course we got to do something like that. All the movies they make have something like that in them. The reason those men got so rich out there is they just make the same movies over and over again. They know what it is you need in a picture.

But listen to this idea. Here's how we keep that girl
from getting me to leave the gospel show. Just
when I'm thinking of going off with her, and
everybody's looking around for me like crazy, then
you just go up to the piano — you know, to keep the
show going — and you start in to singing one of our
songs, and you looking out over everybody's heads
and you're crying a little. That's the real acting part
for you. It isn't hard to cry. What do you mean?
Those people you see with the tears coming
down — those aren't real tears. Didn't you know
that? They got a fellow who comes out with a little
eyedropper and squirts some water on their cheeks
so it looks like they been crying. They got all kinds
of tricks like that. So you at the piano and you crying and you singing one of those songs where I
come in and answer you. Every time it comes to the
place where I'm supposed to answer, there's quiet,
and I know we going to have people out in the audience, they're going to be crying right along with
you. Then they're going to make a cut — that's what
they call it — and they'll show me someplace with
the girl, only I'm hearing your voice, Momma. I
know, I'm outside the church going to get in the car
with her, and she has her arm around me and I'm
looking in her eyes, then I hear your voice, coming
from the distance, with our song.

Now you know I'm not going to hold out long when
I hear you sing. So on the last verse, when you hold-

ing your part extra long, waiting so hard for me to answer you that the whole audience can tell what it is you're feeling, then I come in, very distant, from outside the church. But you hear it, and you start playing the piano faster and looking around and you crying more than ever. I'm telling you, we'll have everybody crying—a boy and his mother, coming back to each other again and staying out of the arms of sin. We can wrap up that scene with me coming down the aisle and everybody standing up and the song coming out with a choir and one of them orchestras they have to fill up the music in the background. You like that? We'll have the fellow come out right after we do a take so he can put the tears in your eyes for you. But I know you, Momma, you going to do that all by yourself.

I even got the ending for the picture now. I don't need to write it down because I'm going to remember it and the Colonel can sell the idea to them out at the studio. The way it ends, the gospel show comes back to the boy's hometown, and he decides to do something special. He says that he's going to do a candlelight confession—that way people won't see him right off—and when everybody comes into the church he turns off the lights except for candles and he makes a long talk for the congregation about how you have to tell the truth, no matter how bad it is, or how much it hurts you, if you want to come to the Lord. And you can hear the boy who really was the cause of the accident, you can hear him start crying. Now I go on and I get worked up a little, and I'm saying that everybody has to say what they've done if they want to come to Heaven, and if they don't there's nothing waiting for them but Hell — and when I start in to talk about Hell then the other boy breaks down all together and starts shouting, "I'm the one, I'm the one who done it. Let this other boy's name be free of any stain, yes Lord, free of any guilt, free of any evil, because I'm the one who drove the car that night. Oh Lord, take away my sin." And he goes down on his knees and the light comes up in the church and everybody sees who it is up there and they wait to see what I'm going to do.

Now comes the moment when we come out with a big song to end it, just like they always do in those pictures. I look at him down there on his knees, and I go down to him, walking as slow as I can. This is the real acting part for me. I go down there to him and I put my hands out and I say, "The Lord will judge you, not me. Rise up sinner, and confess and you will be free." And just then you play a chord on the piano and you start in to singing, and everybody in the congregation will sing it along with you.

What do you think of it? You like the part best when you helping me to wrestle with temptation? That's

the best part then. No, you won't have trouble remembering the verses in the right order when you
singing one of those hymns. They got somebody
standing where the camera can't see him holding
up cards with the words you supposed to sing on it.
That's what I'm looking at when I'm looking off at
something and you think I got my eyes on the girl. I
know you can do it. I don't think we'll have to give
you a new name. I think we can just call you Gladys
Presley. You look so young and cute everybody's
going to say you my sister. You know that's true,
Momma. When they get all that makeup on you,
you won't even know who you are yourself.

But we got to think up a name for our picture. What
do you say we give it the name, "Singing My Song
for You Jesus"? You think there's some hymn with
that name already? How about "Saving It All for
Gospel"? That doesn't get you in it. This is better:
"The Lord's Singing Spirits." That's what I'll call it
for now. But you think that's a good one for us to
begin with?

No, I never seen them pictures. You say there was
some lady out in the woods in Canada and she sings
to some fellow who's in the Mounties? And he
sings some Indian song to her? You can take me to
see them sometime when I come back to Memphis.
If that's the kind of picture you want us to do, then

53

we'll do it. What I want is to do what you want. And we can make up whatever we want for them when we come out to Hollywood. Elvis Presley and his mother crash Hollywood. That's what the magazines will say. You and me, Momma, just like it's always been.

Of course, crazy things happen when you making a picture. You'll have to get used to the things that happen. I never told you about one day when I was doing my first picture. I never did tell anybody, but because of what happened there's a scene in *Love Me Tender* where it's supposed to be me and it isn't, and at the same time there's this cowboy picture they were making — if you look close at it you'll see me in one of the scenes in the barroom.

The way I got into it, there was a boy who was running one of the lights, and he could tell how fidgety I was getting waiting for everything to get set up so I could do my scene. You know how I used to be when I'd go to Sunday school. I couldn't sit still, even when I was listening so hard to what the preacher was saying that I thought I'd bust. When you're making a picture you have to sit so much while they fix up the lights and they get everything they need for the set. Now I had my lines every morning. I didn't never miss. Some of the others — and I won't tell you their names — they'd come in the morning and their hair would be all mussed up and they wouldn't know what scene they were going to do and they wouldn't have any of their lines ready. But for me it was all like a dream coming true, so I was ready no matter when they told me to start.

But all the time, Momma, you still have to sit around, and that used to get me fidgeting in my chair, and when there wasn't nobody around for me to talk to then I wouldn't know what to do with myself. Well, this boy came up to me one morning and he said, "Elvis, there's going to be a big light setup this morning and they won't get around to you for two or three hours." I looked at him and I guess I got a little salty, you know. "What am I going to do for two or three hours?" So he leaned over to me and he said, "You want to be in the cowboy picture?" "Now?" "Sure," he told me, and it seemed like he snuck off whenever they didn't need him, to get into some cowboy clothes and go to the studio next door to get into a scene there.

Now I know I shouldn't have done anything like that, but I could see they didn't need me, and he said he had two cowboy outfits hid away so he didn't have to put the same one on all the time and they wouldn't see that it was him coming back. So we went from one building to the other one, and he had his clothes hanging up in a locker and we changed there back behind the set. I asked him if he didn't think somebody would notice he was gone, but he said they weren't going to be doing anything with his lights until the afternoon, so he was just fidgeting the same as I was.

I wish I could remember the name of the picture they were shooting over there. I could tell my fans to look for me in the scene where there's the fight in the barroom. No, I didn't do any fighting. I was just one of the people who stands in the back of the crowd. The director, he didn't even notice we were there. We come around from the back of the set in our costumes and there's all the rest of the people who are going to be in the scene getting their make-up put on and we stood in line for a little and then we got ourselves looking like all the rest. We didn't have a lot to do. This one fellow was sitting at a table and another fellow comes in the door and we all got out of the way. You know how that goes. We practiced it two or three times and then the director pointed to me. I thought he'd recognized me, you know, but he just said I was tall and people were going to see me, so could I knock over the chair when I got up and then when I bent down to pick it up I'd be out of the way.

There was drinks at the bar, of course, but you know what they drink in those pictures? It's just

tea, Momma. And it's cold. It doesn't taste like anything. So we shot the scene and we all were laughing because it was fun to be dressed up like that and
I didn't want to go back, so the boy who was on the
lights, he knew where there was a phone going
from one studio to the other and he called up and
asked what they were doing where we were supposed to be, and they still were monkeying around
with the lights. That meant we could stay a little bit
more.

Now this is the part that gets funny. There was
some girls doing the scene with us. You know how
those barrooms always have girls who hang
around. They're dressed up in short skirts and
fancy stockings and they got all kinds of beads in
their hair. Well, they gave us a break and two of the
girls went off with us to find a Coke. This was way
off from the set and there wasn't nobody around but
the four of us. One of the girls was drinking her
Coke and she looked at me and she said, "You look
like that singer who's working on the picture over
on the other set." Now the boy with the lights, he
started to laugh, but he saw that I was taking it very
seriously so he held it back and let me talk. "Yes,
ma'am," I told her. "Many people have told me the
same thing." So then she and the girl with her
started talking about it and they decided I looked a
little like Elvis Presley, but my face wasn't quite the

same. The first girl kept it up, and she said, "He's close enough," and then she asked me if I ever tried to do Elvis.

When they say *do* somebody out here, that means you try to act like him. She was asking me if I did any imitations of Elvis Presley. It was getting pretty hard for me to keep from laughing, but I said to her that sometimes I looked in the mirror and tried to do a little Elvis. So you know what they asked me next? — would I sing for them. Of course, the boy with the lights was trying so hard to keep from laughing I thought he was going to explode. His face was all red and he had this funny look in his eyes, like he'd sat down on something hot. I was having some fun with it too, so I put out my arms and sang a little of "Hound Dog." Both of them thought I done pretty good. They really did. So I put a little twist into it and they fell out. The one that asked me to do it said I should get me an agent so I could do some clubs with an Elvis Presley act. Then she asked me if I could do anybody else — you know, do an impression of them, and I said, "No, ma'am."

I could see when I said it that she was a little annoyed with me, but I didn't know what was the matter with her. I went on talking to her, but she started to walk back to the set. So I said, "You don't need to go away," and she turned around and she said, "Don't you know when to stop? It was alright when you were doing your impersonation, but when you go on talking like that it looks like you're just making fun of me." And I could see she was upset. She must have forgotten about the way I was talking when we started out to look for the Coke machine. So I said, "I'm sorry, ma'am. I can't talk any other way."

When I said this I thought she was going to slap me. She stood there with her chest heaving up and down and if she'd had something coming out of her eyes I would have been dead, right there. She couldn't get it out of her head that I was carrying on a joke. Now, you know I don't do things like that. I could see the fellow with the lights, he was going to open his mouth and say something to her, but it was too far gone to make it right so I just started singing again, holding out my arms to her and doing a little bit of "Hound Dog." I figured if she's going to think I'm crazy she might as well think I'm really crazy. When I did that she grabbed her friend's arm and the two of them went back to the set as fast as they could walk in those costumes, and I could hear the first one saying, "That's the kind of jerk you meet out here all the time."

I know, I know, I shouldn't do things like that. But I didn't mean to tease her. I don't never mean to tease anybody. Sometimes things just go a little wrong when I'm not expecting it. If I had told her who I was and what I was doing there — just sneaking off from my own picture — she would have gone along with it. But we had been talking so long I could see we were going to be in trouble ourselves if we didn't get back. So we changed back into our clothes and went across to the studio where we were supposed to be. When I got there I could see they were already doing one of my scenes. It wasn't one where I had any lines to say. I was just supposed to stand on the porch and look for some people to come along. We each of us have what they call a stand-in. You know what that is. They pose in the lights with costumes on so the director can see if he likes the shot. Since I wasn't there they did the shooting with my stand-in. When I come in I said to the man in charge they'd have to do it again now that I was back and he just looked surprised. "I thought that was you all the time. Nobody's going to know the difference, Elvis. In this picture it's not going to make any difference at all."

And you know he was right. I can't tell myself if it's me or not, and after you do everything so many times you can't remember how it's supposed to go and what you supposed to be doing.

No, I'm not saying that it's always so crazy when you're making a picture. When you and me do our picture, Momma, there won't be none of that. When I'm sitting around I'll have you to talk to and I won't get so fidgety.

It was all so new to me, you know, being in Hollywood and making a picture and everything. I still have to pinch myself so I know it's really happening to me. It all shows that you just can't tell what might happen to you in your life. When I went to Mr. Phillips' studio to make that record for you, I didn't have any idea all this was going to happen. I just wanted you to have a present, and the only thing in my mind was learning to be an electrician so I wouldn't have to keep on driving that truck. Remember how I used to tell all those people who were interviewing me, "Yes sir, I was driving a truck when I went in to make that record for my mother, but I was taking a course at the same time so I could be an electrician." I wanted them to know I wasn't just going to be a singer, and I wanted them to know I didn't have to depend on rock and roll to get by. You know when I had to think of the answers to all the questions they asked me — I think I learned more about me than they did.

What you saying? No. You saying that just to help me get over being lonely. You wouldn't want to come on the road with me. Oh I know, we could sit up and talk to each other when it was late, but you wouldn't like some of the things that go on. Besides that, who's going to take care of Daddy Vernon? What do you mean, he can take care of himself. He can't take care of himself, no way. You did every-thing for us all the time, so we never did get used to doing things for ourselves. That's why I always have so many people around me. It takes ten of them to do for me what you used to do all by your-self.

Now, don't you be that way. I'll say things like that if I want to say them. If you don't want to hear them then you can just hang up the phone. You're not going to do that? You're not going to hang up and go to bed? I knew it. You don't have to tell me. I can tell by your voice you still not starting in to get sleepy. I'm not sleepy myself, but I'm starting to get a little crazy. That always happens about this time.

Momma, no, you don't need to worry. It wouldn't do me no good to have you traveling around with me. I'd be worrying so much about the things I was getting you into — all that driving we have to do at night, and all those hotels we check into without ever getting to see if we can sleep in the beds they give us — I wouldn't be able to think about anything else. If I had my mother traveling with me, that would be the first thought in my mind when I woke up in the morning — how can I make it nice for her today? So you stay home. When you come to Hollywood, that's going to be different, but I don't want you to think about coming along with me now.

Did you ever think, Momma, that maybe what I need when I'm on the road is a girl of my own to travel with? I know you thought about it, that's why I said it. What kind of girl would I like to come along with me? I got a girl sitting up with me now who could be the kind of girl I'm thinking of.

Is she pretty? I tell you, she's really pretty. She's as pretty as some of the girls I met out in Hollywood, and she looks a lot nicer than most of them. Maybe I can get her to say hello.

No. She's got all red and she's blushing and she's shaking her head. I think she's too shy to talk to you. What's she look like? She's got pretty brown hair and her eyes — I can't see so well. She's on the other side of the room from me.

You want to come a little closer, honey? I want to look into those eyes of yours.

Don't you get jealous, Momma. I got a whole room full of people here, and they're not going to let anything go on between me and my girl here. Now she's sitting closer, and I can see she's got brown eyes to go with that pretty hair. She's not blushing anymore either, and I can tell you she's got a sweet little smile. You know I like girls that smile like that.

No. The reason you don't hear anybody else is because they all being quiet. My girl's sitting beside me here and we're going to have a cheeseburger and then maybe we'll go off to one of the boy's rooms and sing a little. You know, some of those gospel numbers I like so much. Wait a minute, Momma. Why don't you get yourself another Coke or something, and I'll ask the boys what they're going to do later.

Honey, you see this? When I put the phone under the pillow then nobody can hear anything. You and I haven't had a chance to get acquainted. I can see how pretty you look, but there's more to a girl than just the way she looks. Why don't you try coming a little closer? That's it. And I know you won't mind if I just give you a little kiss.

How about another one? I know you got lots of them there, because you been sitting so patient saving them all up. Oh, that's it. I knew that's the kind of girl you were when I first saw you come in that door.

That's a nice laugh you got, too. That's a very nice laugh, but I bet you can't keep laughing while I'm kissing you. You want to try?

Now if we'd been betting any money you'd have lost, because you didn't keep laughing at all.

You back, Momma? I just put the phone down while I went off with everybody to the other room. They got a guitar in there and they're going to start off without waiting for me to get there. The girl? She's gone off with them. I didn't want anybody listening while I'm talking to you. They don't mind, the boys don't. All of them are used to me talking to you by this time. I've made them stop in some of the craziest places so I could call you up on the telephone and find out how you were feeling.

You beginning to feel a little sleepy now? I can hear it a little bit. Do you remember when I called you from the place where all the guns were going off? You remember that—I called you up so you wouldn't get worried about where I was, and then I told you that all the noise was that bunch of fellows shooting off their pistols, and you got so worried about me you couldn't get to sleep at all. You know we all used to have a lot more fun, but now that it's gotten to be so much money everywhere we have to be careful all the time. I don't remember when it was that I got in with those men, but it was back near the beginning. It was in Louisiana when I still was appearing on the Hay Ride Show. Then I wasn't nearly so big. I was just known in certain sections, but I wasn't known everywhere.

Maybe I didn't tell you everything that happened that time. The boys and them had all checked into the motel and they was thinking about getting themselves something to eat. We had played the night before somewhere — Baton Rouge or Lafayette, one of those places — and we all were feeling pretty tired. It wasn't so late. I was thinking about going down to the swimming pool for a little dip before dinner. I was just starting to take my shirt off when I heard a little knocking on the door to my room. I was thinking to myself it must have been one of the boys, and then I got to thinking they all had keys, so it had to be somebody else. I still wasn't used to people coming to look for me, but I put my shirt back on and I opened the door and there was a girl standing out there. I could see she was about my age, but aside from that there wasn't nothing about her that was the same at all. She was one of those girls who go to different kinds of schools where they have to pay, and she never had worried about what kind of dress she wanted to wear or whether she could buy the kind of shoes that were supposed to go with it. I thought about those kinds of things, from a boy's side of it, but I couldn't do anything about it, and that was the difference between us.

I still can remember the dress that girl had on. It was a sundress and it didn't have any sleeves, but it had a big frilly skirt. It made her look like she'd been out in the sun, because it was all white, but maybe she had been on a vacation. She was the kind of girl who goes on trips like that.

Anyway, she stood there on the balcony of the motel — since we had got put up in rooms upstairs — and she looked very surprised. Then she said, "You're Mr. Presley." I didn't know what she wanted so I said I was, and then she looked at me again. "I went to see your performance last night." Now I figured she was a fan and she wanted me to give her my autograph. But she still stood there and she seemed just surprised. Finally she told me she hadn't expected to see me open the door. "I thought someone like you always had people who did things for him like opening doors. And that they'd keep away the girls who come around looking for you." She had this serious way of talking, but she was so different I didn't know how to answer her so I just said something about the boys being off in the pool and I was going to go after them as soon as I talked to her.

"I know this sounds funny, Mr. Presley." She went on talking the same way. "I sent away to the Sun Record Company for a picture of you and I put it on the wall of my bedroom. I don't know why I did it, since I don't know you at all. Do other girls do that?" I told her that the record company had been getting fan letters asking for pictures, so they knew all about that. "I know a lot of girls put up pictures of movie stars. Do you know why we put them up in our bedrooms?" I just smiled when she said that, the way I always did when a girl started coming on a little bit, but she wasn't doing anything like that at all. "The pictures of people like you go up in our bedrooms because that's the only place we have that's private. The rest of the house is there for everybody and we can't put our own things up."

"But our rooms aren't really private either. Do you know what I mean? My mother or father can come in any time and say what they want."

Now you understand, I was still a little mixed up about what this girl was doing there. It was about five in the afternoon and all the cars were starting to pull into the motel and you could hear all the shouting coming from the pool and I was still all hot and dusty from driving all afternoon. I don't know what I told her. Something about it not making any difference to me if you came into my room and looked at what I had up on the walls.

"My dad came into my room and he looked at your picture for a long time. He said that nobody he ever saw wore his hair like that or had sideburns, and I told him that you were different. And he said he could see that. 'But what kind of a boy is he?' He said that three or four times. 'You have his picture up there on your wall and you don't know anything about him. What kind of boy would go around looking like that?' And I said I didn't know, and he said the next time you were around I should ask you to come over and eat dinner with us. He wasn't being serious, but I said I would do it. And I was being serious. So that's what I came for."

I don't know what I was thinking, but I was tired of all the motels we'd been staying in, and I didn't want to eat another one of those fried chicken dinners at the restaurant, so I told her I'd come with her. I wouldn't do something like that if it happened today, but I knew from the kind of dress she was wearing that it was alright to go to her house. I told her I'd have to go tell the boys, and she came along with me to the pool and the only one that was there was Bill. I told him I was going to eat dinner at the home of a friend, and Bill gave me that look and asked me what was the friend's name. I started laughing because I didn't know her name, but she wasn't upset at all. She introduced herself, and held out her hand and Bill reached up to shake it, forgetting that he was standing in the swimming pool and he managed to splash water on her dress, but not even that seemed to bother her. She just stepped back out of the way, in case he splashed any more water around, and said, "How do you do, Mr. Black. I enjoyed your playing very much last night." Then she remembered she hadn't introduced herself to me and she put out her hand and said, "How do you do, Mr. Presley." I didn't know what to say so I just shook her hand and we went off to her car. I looked back at Bill standing in the swimming pool and he held up his hands to show he didn't understand that girl at all, and I just nodded my head because I didn't understand her either.

I should have known from the car she was driving that she lived in a pretty nice house, but still I didn't know it was going to be that nice. It wasn't so big, but everything in it had a nice look, you know, curtains and everything. What was so funny to me was that everybody was there waiting when we got there. She hadn't called them from the motel, they all must have thought that the most natural thing in the world was for Elvis Presley to come home to have dinner with their daughter.

I thought at the beginning that we were going to spend the rest of the evening standing in the front hall shaking hands, but after they all had called me

Mr. Presley I told them they could call me Elvis and
that made it a little easier. She had a sister who was
a little bit younger, and the lady she said was her
mother didn't look much older than she did. Her
mother was in the same kind of sundress as she
was. Maybe they even traded them back and forth.
They were close enough to each other in size that
they could have done it. Her father was a little big-
ger than me, and I could see he didn't think too
much of having me there, but he was still wearing
his necktie from his work and he still had his suit
coat on. While I was thinking of something to say
the sister said — not trying to be mean or anything —
"You don't look at all like the picture that's up on
her wall." Her sister said she thought I did. I
thought we were going to talk about it some more,
but their father just cleared his throat and the two of
them stopped and waited for him to say something.
He looked at me for a minute and then he said,
"Why don't we go look?"

I know it sounds a little hard to believe, Momma,
but what we did was all of us go upstairs to the girl's
bedroom and we stood there looking at the little
picture of me she had pinned up on the wall. It was
one of those glossy photos that Sun Records was
sending out, and they'd used all those kinds of
lights they had in the photo studio to make it look
like I was romantic. I thought the girl would be a

little embarrassed to have all of us there beside the her bed, but nobody in that family seemed to get embarrassed about anything. She studied the picture for a minute then she looked at me. "I think it looks like him." That's what she said.

Her mother said she thought I looked older in person than I did in the photo. "When was that taken, Mr. Presley — I mean, Elvis?" I told her it had been maybe six months ago and she nodded her head. "I could see some difference. The way someone looks changes so much in those years. Every day my daughters look different, and I'm certain your mother sees just as much change in you." Then when she had said it she smiled at me, just the way you do sometimes.

I was waiting to see what her father would say, and finally he pointed to the eyes in the picture. "I think I would have known it was you from the eyes. But of course, if I didn't notice that, then the hairstyle would give it away. There aren't so many boys we see who wear their hair that way." You know lots of people get real upset about the way I get my hair cut, but it didn't seem to get him mad. It just seemed to be something he'd noticed, like I was wearing a tuxedo, or something like that. Then he asked if I minded a personal question, and I said it was alright, because I was wondering what he wanted to ask me. "Why did you start wearing your hair in that style?"

People ask me that question a lot, but I could see that he really wanted to know, and there we were all standing around that picture like it was something in a museum, so I tried to think of the real answer to give him. "Sir, I usually tell people that I got this kind of a haircut because I wanted to look different for my stage act, but I think one of the real reasons was that I thought it would maybe make me look a little bit older. I tried to grow a beard, but it didn't come to much of anything, so I grew my sideburns instead." Her father just nodded his head and laughed. "I tried to grow a mustache when I was fourteen, but my father kept sending me away from the dinner table to wash the smudge off my face. I know how you feel. Do you want to go eat?" and all of us went downstairs again.

Once dinner started then the daughter just told them all about the concert and my singing and about how she liked to listen to my records, and her mother and father just sat quiet listening, looking over at me sometimes, but mostly watching her face. Her mother sometimes asked me if I liked to be out on the road so much, or if I got tired of being asked the same questions all the time. Usually I just say something like "It's part of being a singer. If anybody is in the eye of the public his life isn't private anymore." But these people all expected me to say what I really felt about things, so you know what I told her? I said to her that those questions she was asking were the ones I got asked over and over. She didn't get upset, she just nodded her head. "But you must understand, your life is so different from the way we live we don't even know how to ask you about what you do."

Their daughter started telling them then about how things had gotten a little out of hand at the theater the night before, with some of the girls trying to get up on the stage, and about somebody pulling the sleeves off my jacket when I went out to get in the car.

"What about that?" Her mother didn't understand it at all. I told her that I accepted all that kind of thing that went on. "None of the girls want to hurt me. They just want a piece of me for a souvenir. That's what it's all about." I didn't think I had said anything that was so funny, but they all began to laugh, and then I could see the joke of it and I laughed right along with them. They could understand the thing that some of these people who write about me never do get — that most of the time I'm just having fun.

After dinner her father asked me if I wanted to come along with him for a little shooting. He was going

off to his gun club and they wouldn't mind if he
brought a guest. Sometimes they had guides or pro-
fessional hunters in from the country, he said, and
they had hair like mine, so nobody would notice. I
asked him what kind of guns and he said it was a
pistol range. Now you know I always liked guns. I
told him I'd be proud to come along with him,
though I didn't know if I'd do any good at it. The two
girls started to say something, since they weren't
going to come along with us, but he said that he'd
bring me back, so they let us go.

What he said about his shooting club was the truth.
There was people there from all over. Some of them
looked like he did and some of them looked like me.
The pistol he had with him was just a little one — a
.22 — but it had a fancy grip and I could see he took
good care of it. "Elvis," he said to me, "do you know
why I like to come out here and shoot a pistol?"

"No, sir." I said, and he just shook his head.

"Damned if I know myself. Why would somebody
like me, who works at a desk all day, want to come
out at night and shoot. I suppose I could make up
some reason about this being my way to get over
being angry at having to sit at that desk all day, but I
think I just like the noise, and I like doing something that doesn't make any sense at all. Everything
else I do makes sense. You can believe that."

Then he handed me the pistol and asked me did I know how to use it. I said I had held a gun a few times, so he asked me to show him how I aimed it, and when I showed him he said we better start at the beginning. Now by this time some of the people there were starting to shoot their pistols. We were in a big room under one of the buildings in town and they had all kinds of soundproofing on the walls, but it still made a lot of noise. It got so noisy in there I was beginning to be afraid something might happen to my ears.

After we'd been doing some shooting — and I didn't do so bad, even if I hadn't been practicing as much as he did — he said he wanted to talk. He wanted to know if I knew what it felt like to have children. He asked me if I had any, and I said, "No, I didn't." We were sitting back in a room away from the shooting, so the noise wasn't so loud, but you could still smell the bullets. You must know that smell from when Daddy Vernon had that shotgun. It stings your nose then it gets in your clothes it's so strong.

He brought us a beer to drink, but you know I didn't want one. We listened to the pistols going off for a little while then he said to me, "I may be the only father around who ever had a chance to talk with the singer whose picture is hanging up on his daughter's bedroom wall. You know, Elvis, somebody like me doesn't know anything about somebody like you. The only thing we see is a picture, and sometimes our daughters play us a record and they get very excited and we try to pretend we understand what it is they're excited about. I don't think they know what it is themselves. It's something about the way you look, the way you sound. Do you ever think about it that much?"

I had to tell him, "No, sir, I don't."

"It's all a little confused, Elvis, because if you're a man you don't understand women very much, and now you have a daughter or two and you think, for a few years, that you do understand something. Everything they do, you know about — they talk to you, they bring things to you, they want you to know who they are. So you feel close to them. And you love them. Let me tell you, Elvis — you're going to find out about this when the time comes — you love them."

Of course, Momma, I could have told him about that. I know how I feel about you, and it's the same thing.

He went on talking, but I didn't mind because I don't get a chance to know what some of these girls' daddies think of me. All I see is those girls screaming up at me when I'm on stage.

"So when you see a picture of some singer or movie star up on your daughter's wall, you realize she's beginning to think about something that doesn't have anything to do with you. In the beginning you don't think too much about it. It's just a sign that she's growing up. But when she begins to talk about the face on the wall so much, then you get jealous. You really do, Elvis, even though you realize it's a silly way to act, you can't help yourself. Certainly you know yourself a lot of parents are disturbed about you, and that's what it's all about. Just think about that. For every girl who jumps and screams at one of your concerts, you've got a man who's jealous, somewhere inside himself—even if he won't tell himself that's what it is. He doesn't like you at all. Do you know what he says to his daughter to get even with you?"

You understand I might not be getting everything just the way he said it, Momma. I couldn't listen all that close, but I was interested in what he was telling me, so that's why I remembered it. He stopped and I could see that he was waiting for me to answer his question. There was so much noise going on I didn't know if I even had heard everything, so I told him "No, sir, I didn't know."

But he still wanted me to answer him. "You think about it. If someone wants to get even with his daughter for talking about somebody who's just a picture on the wall, I'm sure you realize what it is he says to her first."

And I did know what he was talking about. The first thing the grown-ups always said about me was that I wasn't any good as an entertainer. I couldn't sing and I couldn't dance.

He laughed and said that was it and he asked me if I still didn't want to drink the beer, or he'd get me something else if that wasn't what I wanted. He was friendly about everything, and he knew everybody in the place because they all said something to him when they came in, and if they did look at my hair and the way I was dressed, they never said anything because I was with him. "And of course you know what they say about you next." He was asking me a question again, and I knew the answer this time. "They say I'm bad for their daughters. I'm immoral."

"You do understand it, Elvis." He seemed to be happy we could talk about it. "At least for them that's a step along the way. They're not saying you can't sing anymore. What they tell their daughters now is that what you're doing is wrong. Then to finish it up — since I know my own daughters are waiting for me to bring you back — the last thing they say is that you're not going to be popular for long. It's just here today and no one will remember you tomorrow. I'm sure you've heard that."

When I thought about it I remembered all those questions from the people interviewing me, "Don't you think this rock and roll is just a fad?" He was right. And he got me thinking that's the way the people who were writing about me started out. I think that's what they do to you when you first begin to get a little successful — they go through the same things all these girls' fathers do.

It was right then that I noticed what time it was getting to be and I told him I had to call you and he told me where to find a phone. It was in a side office, but I know you could hear everything, and when I told you it was pistols going off I know you got frightened. When I got back he had his pistol all put away and he said we had to drive back, then he did a funny thing as we were leaving. He stopped in the shooting gallery and pointed to some of the men around us who were pretty old. He said to me, "What do you think would happen if I told them you were Elvis Presley? Do you think one of them might be so upset about that music you're doing that he'd turn his pistol your way?" I looked around, but I didn't get scared. I didn't think most of them had ever heard of Elvis Presley. At least not

back then. Everybody's heard something about me
now, but in those days you had to be crazy about
rock and roll to know what was going on. I leaned
over to him and said, "If somebody does aim a pistol
my direction I'm going to point to you and tell him
you're my manager." And that got us both laughing
so hard that two or three people stopped what they
were doing to see what the noise was all about.

After that we got back in his car to drive to his house
again. We talked a little with the whole family,
then the girls said they'd take me back to the motel.
It wasn't so very late when we got there and I still
felt like doing something. I was tired from the driving and my ears were ringing from hearing those
pistols, but it wasn't late and I always did have trouble sleeping. I thought the thing we could do was
go dancing, so I went around to the boys. Bill was
still in his room, so I told him to come along, and we
took the girls to a lounge that was in one end of the
motel. They had one of those country bands doing
ballads and all—it wasn't no rock and roll band,
that's for sure—but we thought we could dance
anyway. Like I said, though, the girls looked very
young, and the man on the door wouldn't let us
come in. The four of us were standing there looking
silly, and the man kept shaking his head. "You two
can come in"—and he pointed to Bill and me—"but
not those two. I can tell just by looking at them that

81

they've got a daddy who would close me down tighter than a baby possum hanging onto its mother's tit if I let them come in here."

He knew who I was and all, and Bill had played in his place a few times before he started working with me, but the man still wouldn't let us in, so I asked him if he would mind opening the back window behind the band, and we could dance on the grass. He laughed at that, but he said it would be alright, and that's what he did. The four of us had our own dance on the lawn of the motel, all by ourselves, back in the trees. We could hear what the band was playing and we could get around on the grass as long as we didn't try any fancy steps. You know, it was like some kind of dream you have when you're a kid. You're dancing with a pretty girl under the trees, and there's music coming from someplace off where you can't see it. After a while the fellows in the band saw us and somebody told them who it was out there, so they moved things around a little so they could sing out to us and finally the one who was doing the singing called out and asked if there was something we wanted to hear, and I told him I liked "Blue Moon over Kentucky" and they played it for us and I sang along in the girl's ear and that's the way the night ended, with us dancing out on the grass with our feet getting wet and that fellow's voice making a little echo where it was all dark around us.

I never told you about that before? I don't know if I thought about it again from then to now. It's crazy the way your mind works. You don't even know you remember something, but then when you start thinking about it everything comes back to you, just like it was happening again. I know you have that happen too.

Oh Lord, what you doing man? You got to stop it and you got to stop it now.

I'm sorry, Momma. Things have gotten a little crazy in here again. Some fellow just come crawling in the door on his stomach and he took my picture with a flash camera. Now I can't hardly see him with the glare still in my eyes.

Man, I don't want to see you in here. You put that camera down before I throw it out the window.

Just a minute, Momma. I got to put the phone down.

You look now, man, you got all day to do that. I give all those press conferences and I stand around doing the damnedest dumb things so you all can get some kind of picture, and that's all I'm going to do. How'd you get in here anyway? You could be one of those guys that sends me a letter saying that his girl doesn't like him now that she's seen me on the stage and he's going to come and shoot me.

You going to get out? If you don't and I call the boys, they going to take you out and you don't want that to happen. Okay, you say they're drunk, but they just get meaner when they're drunk.

I'm telling you, I said out. I know I let people like you come and do what you want sometimes, but you pushing it, you know? You look behind you — that's the door you come in, and that's the door you're going out. You crawled in here and you can go back out the same way. You take another picture of me or of that lady and I'm going to throw you out the window along with your camera.

Out of here. That's what I'm telling you.

No, Momma, I didn't need any help. You heard all of that? Those people are so crazy. I give them everything when I'm out on the stage. I dance for them, I love up the microphone for them, I sing those songs over and over again for them. But it still isn't enough. They have to come crawling into my room to see if they can't get some more.

I didn't mean you, of course.

I'm talking to the girl who's still here with me.

You don't listen to any of that, Momma. You don't pay it any attention. I get to laughing over it myself. I can't take it so seriously as all that. I get to my hotel and I look down at the street and there's all those girls standing there shouting, "We want Elvis! We want Elvis!" and I don't know what they're doing out there. No, I really don't.

I look at all that going on and I think maybe I should go around to the houses where they live. You know what would happen if I did that. I'd go around to where they live and I'd stand in the middle of the street and start to shouting up at the windows, I want Jean! or I want Audrey! or I want whatever her name is! and you think people would just laugh about it, like I do? No, that's right. They'd come and arrest me. They'd send a police car down the street to pick me up, and it wouldn't do any good for me to say I was just getting even for all those girls doing the same thing to me.

It's nothing new. Just two sets of rules. I have to go by one set of rules and my fans can go by a different set. I think that's why some of the guys I meet in show business get so mixed up. They don't ever understand about this. You know, somebody should print up our rules for us. When a singer gets a gold record or appears on a big TV show then he should get a little book in the mail. *Rules for How To Get Along If Your Face Is Known a Little Bit.*

That's right, Momma. They'd have to send us a different book if we had two gold records. And somebody like me, they'd have to make up a whole new rule book, because I can't go anywhere without people knowing my face. You come to accept that like it is, but I don't think there's anybody else who understands that I can't live like other people. That's what I need my rule book for. Since I don't have a book telling me what to do, I have to keep remembering how I'm supposed to act now I'm a star, but when I don't have time to think about it then I make mistakes.

Of course, if you're an Elvis Presley fan you can do anything you want without somebody thinking it's a mistake to act that way. Most of the time they got their mothers and fathers telling them, that's their mistake — being fans of Elvis Presley. What did that magazine say about me? — "the biggest menace to young people in America today." If you're a fan of somebody like that then you really making a mistake!

You're not sleepy yet, Momma? I can see my little girl here is having trouble keeping her eyes open.

You're beginning to feel a little bit tired? I know I'm starting to feel it when I can't keep my mind on what I'm saying. But it still might be an hour before I can go to bed and fall off to sleep.

Was I upset by all that was going on in the room? No, I never get worked up over that, even if it's somebody crawling down the hall to take my picture. You know the way we do it at home. If the fans can keep quiet and stay out of everybody's way then they can stay around. It's like I always say, God gave me this talent, and if I forget how to be nice to people He's going to take it away.

I know it does get bad down there in Memphis. I can't even take one of the cars to the gas station without a half-dozen jokers tailing me or going on ahead on their bikes like I needed an escort. The only times I get in trouble is when I got a bunch of them hanging around me. When I'm on the road, like I am now, then I'm out in the public anyway, so they all want to see what I'm doing. Nobody would say anything in those articles about the kind of food I eat if I could do all my eating home with you. It's when I go out to a restaurant that they start saying things.

I think sometimes about why I go on doing it. After tonight I suppose I'm going to have to go around the country so people can see the rest of me, not just the half that Mr. Sullivan put out on his show. But since the movie's out now and anybody can go see it anytime he wants to, I don't have to go on traveling like this. If I make it big in the movies I might just quit and do that instead, but it isn't only money that I'm thinking about when I'm driving along those highways. When I first started out singing I was traveling all the time. You remember how it was. I wasn't making any money, but I wanted to be out there anyway. What I think is true, and I know some of those other boys like Jerry Lee or Carl—those boys from Sun—if you asked them they'd say the same thing. You out there because you want people to look at you and listen to what you doing.

No, I don't mean it that way at all. That isn't it. I don't know any of the guys singing rock and roll who want people to look at them because they're good looking. Or at least they think they're good looking. They want people to say, "I know who he is. I know about that boy!" You always have a dream that if you using the right song or if you get the right arrangement or if you do some old song in a new way that catches on, then everybody's going to listen. I never met a singer who didn't think about it the same way. That's what we're trying to do. We want everybody to know we're here. "Listen to me, you all. Listen to me." That's what we're singing.

If we really get the song right, Momma, then even the children of the people listening to it today, their children are going to listen to our records. Some of those boys at Sun, they listened to Jimmy Rodgers records. They knew about him even when he was gone. It's going to be the same thing with the records we making now, and when those kids listen to what we're saying they're going to hear that same thing over and over. They're going to hear us saying, "Listen to me. That's what I want from you. I want you to listen to me!"

A record producer I ran into in the studio, we were sitting waiting for the band to get through rehearsing and he told me he had a dream about making a record that would be so good everybody in the country would have to run out and buy it. You know, he'd get something into the arrangement that nobody had ever thought of before, and he'd have people standing in line to buy the record.

Of course, you're right—that's what happened to some of my releases—but in his dream the record is so good everybody in the United States has to buy it. It's the biggest hit anybody ever had in all music history. But what comes next is that he does another record that does just as good. Everybody's standing in line to buy this record just like they did the first one. And he keeps it up. He's a hit man. He knows just what everybody wants to hear. Now this big hit man, he doesn't want to stop. He's made so much money he could do something else, but he wants to keep his hits coming. This is all this fellow's dream. No, we never did do a record together, but maybe we should have.

Now he goes on making his records, and people can't stop buying them. So what happens? People run out of shelves to keep their copies of his records on. They start to pile the records up on their floor, then that space runs out and they have the records piled up in their attics and finally that gets to be too crowded and they have the records piled up in the backyard. This is where he gets in trouble, because the government has to do something. Congress passes a law saying he can't make any more records. Anytime he goes out of the house he's got a policeman following him so he can't get into the recording studio, and he has an idea for his biggest hit, one of those sweet-sixteen numbers — "Linda, Could You Be the First?" by The Glow Socks, or "Beginning Is Better Than Starting over Again" by The Dynamophones, something like that — and he can't do it. So he goes on television and makes a pledge that for the sake of his country he won't make another pop single and Congress has a special medal designed just for him and the President pins it on him at a special ceremony at the White

House — just like they're going to do to me some-day — and his name goes into all the history books for kids to study in school.

That was that fellow's dream. All of us have a little of the same dream. You too, Momma, only you want everybody to buy my records and nothing else. If I couldn't dream about something like that then I couldn't accept some of the things that happen to me. I couldn't accept being so far away from you and Daddy Vernon. I couldn't accept sitting up in this hotel room while the girl waiting for me is getting so sleepy I can see her eyes closing down on her, no matter what she does about it. I couldn't accept living where everybody looks at me all the time like I was in the zoo.

What's my own dream about being a star? You know about my dreams. Those years when Daddy Vernon was gone and we slept in the bed together I always used to tell you my dreams when I'd wake up. But the dreams I have now, they're different kinds of dreams. I think I'd keep on doing what I'm doing. If I had to choose what I'd do in my dreams I think it would just be to go on singing like I am now, except I think I'd get some different costumes. You know how I like to pick out what I'm going to wear. Suppose I let go and put on all the things I really think about. All kinds of capes and spangles and high collars like they had in the old days. Wouldn't I look good? Like some kind of king. The King of Rock and Roll. They call me that anyway, so I might just as well dress up so I look like it. Then when I do my shows I'll have a whole orchestra to back me up, not just the combo, and I can come on stage with my cape swinging around my shoulders.

That's my dream of what I would look like. I'd have to have some kind of baton to go with it. Kings always carry something in their hand. I know what it could be, Momma! I could carry a flashlight so I could see people's faces when I'm up on the stage and everything's shining in my eyes so I can't see anything. What would people say if I came out on the stage dressed like that?

You wouldn't laugh? I don't know how many people would laugh, but most of the time you see somebody dressed like that on stage you think they're a magician or something like that. That's what I could do. I could come out like I was the King and I was going to do a song, but when I opened my mouth a bird would come out instead of words. I could have a whole string of birds like that, all different colors, and I could make the audience guess what song I was singing by the colors of the birds. Then when I was dancing I could swing the cape around the microphone so it would look like a woman was up there, too, then I'd have somebody to dance with.

But you know, I'd come out like that, with my fancy costume and I'd do all my tricks, and they'd still make me sing "Hound Dog" so I could get off the stage. That's the way it is when you dream something.

My real dream? My real dream. You know what that is. Someday I'm going to find the right girl and I'm going to stop this running around the country and I'm going to stay quiet with her and I'm going to have a family. Kids. I don't know how many I'm going to have, but she and I can decide about that after. I think about that a lot. Maybe it's the same dream everybody has, but there's no reason I can't have it too. And part of it is just going off to be alone with her and living close to you at the same time so I wouldn't have to give up anybody I love. I do dream about that. What would it be like to go back to being simple? Maybe I could finally finish that course I started on being an electrician. Instead of doing all this crazy kind of thing I'm doing now I could get a truck and drive around doing electrician jobs and nobody would say anything about who I was or how I was wearing my hair.

You know every time I look in the paper there's somebody else from high school talking about how they knew me so well, and I never even heard half their names. If I was just an electrician and somebody asked them if they remembered me they'd say, "Elvis who? I never heard of anybody named Elvis."

Now we're talking about dreams, I have another one. It's a dream about when I'm such a big star that everywhere in the world people know who I am, and I can do a TV program and it will go out on a station everywhere and I'll be in front of a big audience in some place like a football stadium or something. My dream is that when I get everybody looking at me to see what I'm going to do I'll hold out my hands, and what I'll say is, "Now we're going to pray. We're going to pray to Jesus, because without him we don't have anything at all."

It is funny, like you say, that I dream of being simple again and I used to dream all the time of being a star. But I get so crazy sometimes when I talk to people and they think I'm so famous that they just look at me. They don't even think they're supposed to answer anything I say, or if they do, they're trying so hard to say something I'll like. I don't know what I'm doing when I talk to them. I get kind of lost because it's just like I'm looking in a mirror—everything I do, they do. You know how kids in school will sometimes watch their teacher's mouth, and they'll mimic him, talking at the same time he does, and after a little while he gets so mixed up hearing his words coming back to him at the same time with a sound he's not used to that he stops talking. That's what happens to me. I finally stop because I don't know what to do next.

Then the other kind of thing happens to me. When you get famous everybody has an idea in their mind of what you're supposed to be like. You know, they've read all about me in the fan magazines and they've read somebody's interview and they think they know all about me. Then they meet me and I start saying something a little bit different and it seems like they don't even hear it. They go on just like I was something in a magazine. I can do my best to make them listen, but they know what Elvis Presley's supposed to be like and if I say something different then I can't be Elvis Presley. It's like Elvis Presley is only a name and it would be a lot easier if I was just made out of cardboard and they had a recording stuck behind the cardboard saying the things everybody expects me to say. That's all they want from somebody who's a star. Maybe that's how you get to be a star — giving people what they expect from you every time, and you don't dare be anything different.

It scares me sometimes, all the different ways people act when they find out who I am. It's like I'm going in and out of different rooms, and every room I go into, people think I'm somebody else. I get lost myself, wondering which one of those people I really am.

How you doing, honey? That's it. Let me see those pretty eyes of your again. I thought you were going to sleep for a minute, but you were just listening. You could tell all your girlfriends you heard Elvis Presley's secrets. But you wouldn't tell them, would you? I know Momma's going to go to sleep soon, and I can feel my own head beginning to go around. Can you go find us some more Cokes? I feel my throat going all dry from this talking.

Just one minute before you go off. I think I could have a kiss before you go off. Everybody's gone off somewhere, so if I'm going to get a kiss, you got to be the one that gives it to me. Just like that. Now you hurry back.

I'm sorry, Momma, I didn't mean to cut you off, but I asked my girl to go get us something to drink to keep my throat from getting so dry. She's going to go home right after. I don't need nobody to stay around, and one of the boys'll be staying in the room with me anyway so I don't walk off in my sleep. It's crazy how that happens. I know you told me that everybody in the family's been doing it all their lives, but I still don't understand it. The girl that's been sitting here with me will go home as soon as she brings me something. I know she's got somebody waiting to take her home anyway. Like I said, she's not like those other girls who hang around here. I can tell just by looking at her that she's a nice girl.

You know, Momma, if you go to sleep now, then you can help read all those letters I been getting when you wake up tomorrow. I know some of those letters are going to be for you anyway. You already got a bunch of them. Once somebody gets to be famous then people think they can be personal with him, and if they want to write a letter to his mother they go ahead and do it. We been getting letters addressed to my cats, and you remember when there was that story about me liking teddy bears and we got so many of them in the mail we didn't know where to put them.

I suppose I should get upset about how foolish all those people are acting, but it isn't really me they're sending things to. They have some idea about me that's really just about what they'd like to be themselves. When they send me something it's because they'd like to get something from somebody, and they give it to me instead. I think that's what's happening. Didn't you ever want to send a letter or a

97

little present to Clark Gable? I thought everybody did back when he was such a big star.

I think the funniest part of those letters is what they want to know about. They ask me all kinds of things. I get the same thing when I do interviews for some of the fan magazines. When I'm talking to them I say whatever comes into my mind, because I know it's all going to come out alright. You know I wouldn't say anything that would get anybody worried, but they ask me all kinds of questions and I can't answer them sometimes. Like I said, when somebody comes to be in the public eye then there isn't anything about him that's private. That's just facing the facts. So they ask me all kinds of things. You know the kinds of questions I mean. That's right. What kind of girls do I like and where do I want to go when I get tired of rock and roll and what do I want to do with all the money I'm making.

I always give them some kind of answer. I can go any which way they want me to go. I know about those kinds of things. But then they think because I'm so popular I must know about other kinds of things that go on too — about what's happening in America and what do I think about all the new ideas coming into people's minds, and do I want the coloreds to get ahead. All kinds of things like that. And I tell them, you ought to ask somebody else questions like that—somebody who knows about things like that—because I don't know about all those kinds of things. But you know what they say? Nobody wants to hear what any of those other people think about things. They might have the answers, but nobody's interested in what they have to say. So those people doing the interviews come and ask me. Now I think that's kind of foolish to ask a rock and roll singer about things like the country or what people should do with their lives. What do we know? I spend all my time listening to music and doing my show. I don't say I shouldn't have been paying more attention to other things, but at the time I didn't have any of that on my mind.

I think you and Daddy Vernon could tell these people more than I could. I'm not being shy about it. That's what I really feel. Somebody like me, he's so young and he hasn't been out in life the way you have. The kind of life we lead when we're out on the road, it's so crazy sometimes I don't think they could get an answer out of us about anything. But they come asking all those questions and you have to answer them because they say they're going to write something for the fans or they're going to broadcast what you're saying over the radio. What could I tell them—all about the last place down the road we stopped for gas, or how dirty it was in the dressing room where we played last night? If I did tell them something like that they wouldn't pay it no mind. They think because I'm famous now I can tell them anything, but I think if people go to a rock and roll singer to find out what they need to know in life then those people are going to get themselves into trouble.

That's right, Momma. You shouldn't try to read all the things people are saying. Just look at the pictures. Some of them are pretty good. I like the ones where you can see what I'm doing up on the stage and you can see the faces of the girls at the same time. You can tell just what it is they're feeling. Those people who do the interviews always ask me if I like the way the girls carry on, and I tell them I accept it all with my mind open, because that's the way people are. You know those cartoons they have at the picture shows, when the boy rabbit — or the bird or the cat or whatever it is — sees a girl rabbit. He jumps up and down and gets all red in the face and then he does some kind of crazy thing like running into a fence.

That's what's going on when those girls try to get up on the stage with me, and they try to bite me and scratch me. If I was sitting down there and some girl was up on the stage doing what I'm doing, I'd start screaming and I'd want to get up there with her just like they do. Whatever it is that happens I'll just go on doing my best to please everybody, so you just don't pay any attention to all the things people write or Mr. Sullivan just showing me from the waist up. That doesn't matter one way or another. It's just in one ear and you forget about it a minute later.

Some of these guys that want to write about me, they get real salty about it sometimes. I can see what they're thinking — here's this guy who's just come up out of nothing and now he's real famous all of a sudden and I have to write about him to hold on to my job. They don't only do it to me. I can tell what they're thinking when they go around to the other people singing on the shows and they ask them the same questions they just got through asking me. They don't like to see nobody doing a new thing that they can't get in on. So they don't write about what I'm doing. They just write about what they think I'm doing. And it gets pretty hard to write about that because the way it is on the shows now the girls are screaming so much I can't tell what I'm doing myself. Like I say, I can hear what's going on for maybe five seconds while the announcer says my name, and then it gets so loud out there I could be singing them a song about Grandpa Jessie's hogs and it wouldn't make no difference. But those people have to write something for their newspapers or their magazines, so they talk about the way I'm looking at people or the way I'm moving my legs.

I know if I keep on being famous somebody's going to come along and write something about me that's going to be real mean. I can see it when these guys talk to me. Something about me gets them madder than a hornet. What I'm doing up on the stage, when I walk around like that, what I'm doing is all the things they wish they had the nerve to do. Everybody would like to carry on like that. But they don't do it because they get afraid somebody will laugh at them. Well, I went out and did it, and some people laughed, but I didn't get discouraged by that and I kept going. So now anybody can come along and do the same thing and they won't get laughed at. These guys are all the ones that wanted to be something a little bit different, but they were afraid, and they get all upset with me because I didn't let something like that stop me. I wasn't afraid about anything and that got them feeling jealous. That's what I can see in their eyes when they're talking to me. All I can tell them is that's the way it's always been and that's the way it's always going to be.

Now whoever it is comes along and writes something real bad about me, you know he's not going to write about what I'm doing up on the stage, or about my singing, or the music we do. He's going to write about all the other things that go on, about how the boys get a little drunk sometimes or about how we all like to party every now and then. And he's going to write about me personal. He's going to say I'm not so good looking up close and I didn't do so good in school and we was real poor when I was growing up. I know sometimes they want to do an interview with me at ten o'clock in the morning and I get out of bed and I don't have time to get myself looking good or shaved or anything. And then we don't have our clothes ready because they're still in the car and I haven't had but a couple of hours to sleep because we been driving all night. But I go down to see this person and we start in doing the interview and I can see him saying to himself, this Elvis, he ain't so much when you get him up in the morning. Then I think, unh-huh, that's going to go into somebody's book sometime.

But whoever this person may be, he won't be able to say anything about what happens when I come out on the stage and all those people begin screaming. Because that's dreams, Momma, that's their dreams. And you can't say anything about people's dreams. When the lights come on and the music starts and I go out there and start singing, that's my dream. So it doesn't matter if somebody wants to say things about how I treated some girl or my high school grades or whether I had my shoes tied when I come down the stairs in the motel — that isn't dreams. As long as the dreams go on, it don't matter one little bit whatever any of those people want to say about me.

Now I know your time's different there and it's an hour earlier in Memphis, but you got to get a little sleep. You got to take care of yourself. I'm going to be getting into bed myself as soon as I hang up. You go to sleep now, Momma, you hear. I'm thinking of you, just like I always do. You know all about that because it's been that way all my life. It's you I'm thinking about when I go to sleep, and it's you I'm thinking about the first thing when I wake up in the morning. I'm going to be back home in a few days and I can tell you about it myself. Wherever I am tomorrow night I'll call you again. You know that. Goodnight now. Goodnight, honey.

Now I forget what they told me your name was. Betty, or Peggy. Betty? Well, whatever your name is, you're the one, baby. You're the one I been thinking about all the time. You been sitting over there so patient. Why don't you come a little closer and you can rub my back while I get a little something to eat. I like what you're wearing. I really do, honey, but don't let me stop you if you want to get into something a little lighter. Now just let me lie quiet a little and you can tell me about yourself. I always want to know just what kind of girl it is that would get herself worked up over a guy like me. And you just don't pay any mind to what I'm doing while you're telling me . . .

COLES
TO
JERUSALEM